INTERPRETATIONS *of* LOVE

Also by Jane Campbell

Cat Brushing

JANE CAMPBELL

INTERPRETATIONS *of* LOVE

A NOVEL

Grove Press
New York

First published in Great Britain in 2024 by Riverrun, an imprint of Quercus Editions Limited.

Printed in the United States of America

First Grove Atlantic hardcover edition: August 2024

Typeset by CC Book Production

Library of Congress Cataloging-in-Publication data is available for this title.

ISBN 978-0-8021-6288-5
eISBN 978-0-8021-6289-2

GrovePress
an imprint of Grove Atlantic
154 West 14th Street
NewYork, NY 10011

Distributed by Publishers Group West

groveatlantic.com

24 25 26 27 28 10 9 8 7 6 5 4 3 2 1

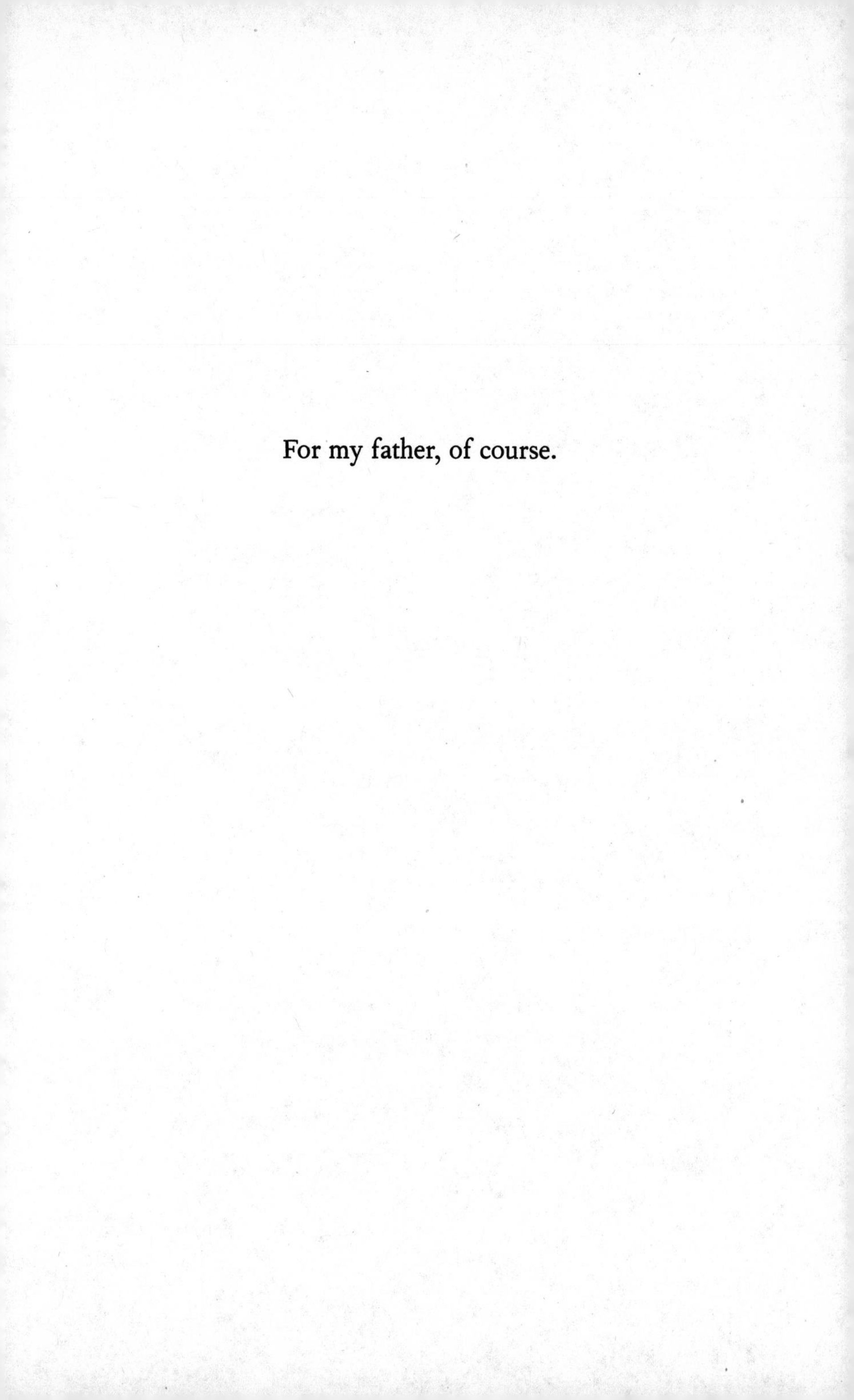

For my father, of course.

INTERPRETATION The process of elucidating and expounding the meaning of something abstruse, obscure, etc.

LOVE Psychoanalysts have as much difficulty defining such a protean concept as do others.

A Critical Dictionary of Psychoanalysis,
Charles Rycroft, Penguin Reference, 1986

It would take too long to explain the intimate
alliance of contradictions in human nature
which makes love itself wear at times
the desperate shape of betrayal.
And perhaps there is no possible explanation.

A Personal Record, Joseph Conrad

PROFESSOR MALCOLM MILLER

The day before the Wedding Reception

I AM AN OLD MAN now, older than my years. I drink too much and find reasons not to exercise, not to socialise (ghastly word, my apologies). I love no-one, or almost no-one, not any more. I exist in a sort of tepid slurry of dissatisfaction with myself and my life. Now and again a brief twang of desire for a specific pleasure echoes through me; could be sex, could be a new idea, could be a few stirring chords on a piano. But nothing persists. I am soon able to turn away and slouch back to my familiar toad-like existence. That too, I am hideous now. Layers of mottled superfluous skin lie around my neck, and my eyes, behind my glasses, are moribund. I am sitting here in my comfortable apartment on the second floor of the rather classy little housing unit built for us Oxford academic oldies looking out at the view of the charming twelfth-century church, St Ethelburga, and its assortment of ancient gravestones. Inevitably, such a reminder of the eternal verities can easily ruffle one's ordinary, hard-held complacency and I have been meditating, as I do often these days, on some of the significant choices made by me in the past.

Of all the truths I have garnered from my long and rather unsatisfactory life I think the most durable and the most alarming is the promiscuity of our perceptions. Faithless disciples, our eyes are, but even more than our eyes, our subsequent deductions, our rambling conclusions, our firm convictions, will go to bed with anyone, any thought, any image, and swear in the morning that it did happen, or, actually, it did not happen. They were not there. We were not there. We saw nothing or we saw everything. It was good, it was bad. It was simply marvellous. We need no new landscapes but only new eyes. We believe what we see but first, we decide what we will see. Not consciously, of course, but secretly, deviously, leaving no compromising fingerprints. And the engine of all this deception? Our appetites. Our infinite hunger. Our ghastly fears. There is nothing new in this perspective. Miniature Tantaluses (or would that be Tantali?) we are surrounded by delicious and gratifying delicacies without any hope of ever reaching them and, only if we could see them as the empty and worthless trivia that they are could we then resist the yearning for them and live peaceful, calm, sated and presumably happy lives? But how dull. How infinitely tedious that would be. Do you not agree? And I realise I must make something clear: I speak of people, not things. Of emotions, of loves and hates, of our sentient responses to that vast cluster of human beings whom in the course of the average life we will encounter along the way. I have tried to acquire indifference on this long journey. I have failed but I have done my best. I am nearly there. My age helps.

Who or possibly what am I? I would describe myself as a retired Oxford don, a former Professor of Old Testament Studies at Pembroke, a crusty old bachelor with a dicky heart. There are other variations of me along the corridor and a decent wine list downstairs in the communal dining-hall. Sally, the newest and sweetest of the care staff, seems to have adopted me as her special pet and I do not protest.

Why then should you care about the story I am about to tell? The answer is short and to the point. It is not, or I did not think it was, in the end, about me. I speak as the messenger, the observer, the prompter, and although I have more or less driven this old skill of mine into the ground, I can still form a sentence, still find a verb, still nail down the iridescent adjective which will transform a squalid mud puddle into gold. So, here goes.

My story is about a letter. The letter, which is propped up

there on the windowsill, was given to me some fifty years ago by my elder sister Sophy. On the envelope is written in my sister's elegant longhand, 'Dr Joseph Bradshaw. Private and Personal'. It was written in the summer of 1946 when I was almost twenty and after Sophy had established that Joe had survived the war and just before she and her husband Kurt went off to a little holiday cottage practically on the beach just south of Merebridge for a few brief and happy days with four-year-old Agnes. How effortlessly we made our plans. How confidently.

After the three of them had spent a few days there I would drive my old Morris Eight the few miles down the Wirral coast and hand over the car and they would then drive on to Chester and I would bring Agnes home with me. Scanning the Dee Estuary again when I drove down had reminded me of the reassuringly austere and unregimented outlook all along that coast. Sophy and I had grown up in Merebridge, on the edge of this vast stretch of undulating brown sand with nothing but glimpses of the Irish Sea beyond and the shadow of the Welsh mountains there on the horizon. When I look back what I remember is the utter peace of it all and, as I drove, my eyes dwelt lovingly on the familiar rocks fissured like old skin and on the grass-lined dunes beside them as I listened to the wind full of the seagulls' cries. That day Sophy had been so happy and sparkly and indiscreet. 'Honestly, Mally, I think we made love ALL night!' And she grinned and wriggled and I thought I had never seen her so full of life and joy. I handed the car over to them, 'the engine of death' as I rather dramatically termed it to myself later on, and then travelled back home on the train with little Agnes. 'Have you delivered the letter, Mally?' Sophy had whispered and I had sort of half-nodded, sort of half-shaken my head for of course I hadn't, being a well-practised procrastinator, but I knew I would and so I had said, 'Don't worry.' I had planned to do it the very next day; however, by then everything had changed.

The farewell to Agnes was not a good one. She was sitting on the rocks watching Sophy in her Sunday best walk along the sands towards the ramp up to the road where Kurt was waiting when suddenly she ran after her mother, crying, shouting, 'Don't go Mummy. You might drown.' She must have thought Sophy was walking into the sea and it may have been partly Sophy's fault that she had this misapprehension as her mother had warned her again and again not to go too far while the tide was out since she had heard that it would come in with the speed of a galloping horse: just the kind of detail Agnes would always remember. 'Don't leave me alone,' shouted Agnes, but she was not alone; I was there. Sophy had kissed her goodbye. 'Uncle Mally will look after you. I'll be back soon,' Sophy had called. 'Be good.'

So I took Agnes back with me on the train. I had never

spent much time with her before this but I was today her only protector and she allowed me, with absolute trust, to fulfil that role. She sat on my knee and we peered together out of the window down into the back gardens of the small houses we passed and looked for the quick glimpses of the sea that we could sometimes make out between them. She smiled at everything, and when we stopped at the small station platforms along the way I opened the window and she stood on the seat and leant out while I put my arm around her tiny delicate body and then she collapsed back onto my knee when the train started again. 'I saw him waving his flag and blowing his whistle, Uncle Mally.' How vividly a child's face can radiate happiness, I thought, and I had never known that. And, in a curious way I felt both proud and enormously touched by her presence. 'Mummy and Daddy will be back soon,' she confided to me.

When we arrived at Merebridge it was a short walk along Stanley Drive to the vicarage and I took her hand but I could see that she was tired and suddenly she stopped and lifted up her arms and said, 'Please carry me Uncle Mally.' And so I picked her up, so light, so small, and she put her arms around my neck and her cheek on mine. 'I love you, Uncle Mally,' she said and I of course responded, 'And I love you too Agnes.'

I found I was walking with such care. Every step I took along the wide sunny pavement through the shadows of the lime trees was freighted with significance for I was carrying this incarnation of innocence. I was suddenly aware of the unknown life with all its terrors and excitements that stretched ahead of her and resolved to look after her forever. When we got home and I had, with some reluctance, handed Agnes over to my mother, it was tea-time and then my mother bathed Agnes while my father and I started a game of chess which we never finished. Almost at once he had a phone call to say that there had been a car crash, Kurt was dead and my sister was seriously injured and in Chester Memorial Hospital. My father drove us to Chester. Sophy was dying and he gave her the last rites. I did not know what to do or where to look. I mainly remember not wanting to be there. She knew in so far as she knew anything that Kurt was dead and she was talking incoherently about Joe and Agnes and I am not sure any of it made sense to my father but it did to me. 'You delivered it,' she said to me at one stage and of course I nodded. 'Yes, Sophy.' 'Then he'll have it.' She died soon after. On the way back, I drove my grief-shattered father while he sat with his head in his hands, maybe praying, and I watched the headlights on the road and thought of the letter still in my room at home.

When we got back Agnes was tucked up in bed upstairs, knowing nothing of all this, while my parents and I had whispered, subdued, weeping conversations about what to do. At some stage I said, 'I need to get back to college,' and neither of my parents questioned this.

In the morning I woke to an unnaturally quiet house. In the sitting room I found Agnes and my mother side by side on the sofa. Agnes had her legs drawn up and was fiddling with the tops of her ankle socks while my mother was making useless gestures with her hands and saying, 'Stop fidgeting, Agnes.' Agnes's face was white, her eyes wide, her mouth twisted as though she had been fed something disgusting. 'Uncle Mally,' she said, 'I need my mummy.' She struggled off the sofa and ran towards me and I could see that her eyes were suddenly filled with hope: I was the person to whom her mother had entrusted her only yesterday, we had shared such joy on our train journey, I had carried her home when she was tired, I was large and strong and I would know how desperate her need was. It was all clearly there in her eyes for me to read.

I turned away and walked into my father's study where I found him with his head buried in his arms on the desk.

'Dad,' I said. 'Someone has got to do something about Agnes. Mother can't cope.'

He stood up and walked ahead of me into the sitting room where he picked Agnes up and as her head drooped onto his shoulder she began to weep, her voice echoing around the house, escalating into an utterly mournful sort of wail. I watched my father holding her, patting her back, as I turned away and went upstairs to collect my bags and the letter. 'Goodbye,' I called from the hall, 'I'll be back.'

Did I really do such cruel and heartless things? Maybe my memory is too damning. The emotion I remember most vividly from that time was fear. The shame came later. Then it was fear of the abysses of sorrow that I could see opening up around me. Fear of some sort of contamination of grief that would drag me down with it. I told myself there were, of course, mitigating circumstances. She was only a child. She would, surely, forget. I had been only a very young man, barely a man, when it happened. But no, there were no mitigating circumstances: boys my age had been dying in battle for years. I had walked swiftly to the station, thinking of an essay I was due to prepare, shoving sentences around in my head and at the station I bought a newspaper and buried myself in its pages and crosswords and then when I was back on the train to Oxford I got a journal out of my briefcase that I was editing and started to mark it up. Agnes and her terror slowly disappeared behind a mist of words. This was my reliable nostrum. By the time I reached Oxford I felt almost normal.

What sort of man would behave like that in Agnes's hour of need, I ask myself, as I pick up the letter and take it out of the envelope.

Earlier this morning I had lifted Volume II (P–Z) of the *Compact Edition of the Oxford English Dictionary* down from the shelf by my desk. Once, as Fellow Librarian at Pembroke, I had unimpeded access to the whole college library but now I had to make do with these three volumes, although this was no small matter as each volume weighed several pounds. I soon found, after a bit of fumbling with the pages and manhandling of the magnifying glass (provided with the set), the word I needed. Remorse.

Well, I said to the open page before me, you may consider 'a remorse' obsolete but it is a very real and present and immediate problem for me. I examined the page with affection. In order to be able to compress so much learning into so small a space an extremely small print had been used and my hand rested on the page as I held the magnifying glass over the tiny illegible letters. The feel of the fine, white paper beneath my palm pleased me. A familiar sensory accompaniment to my years as a scholar. Barely able now to do more than imagine the thrill of a yet undiscovered word that in time might lie so snugly in my memory.

I raised the magnifying glass again. *1605* (Temple) *Hist. Eng. (1699) 578 'Either the Fame of his Forces, or Remorse of his Duty, prevailed with Duke Robert to offer again his submission.'* Remorse of his Duty. How horribly appropriate. '*Her conscience remorsed her and she fyl doun to hir feet requyryng pardon.*' Amazing how much hadn't changed, I thought, examining the old spellings. And the feeling, the remorse, the desiring of pardon, that did not change either.

I cannot escape forever. I am sitting here now reflecting with shame on that extraordinary moment of cowardice in my life. A scholar can always escape into his own small intellectual universe and I was always a scholar. It has been so easy to disappear into my study, to lose myself in my novel reading of Exodus 17:8–16 in light of the Heliopolitan Cosmogony, or to hide behind any one of a number of pressing academic expectations such as the revisions of HG May's Oxford Bible Atlas. All over now. I pick up the letter which I know almost by heart.

The Vicarage
23 Stanley Drive
Merebridge
21 July 1946

Dear Joe,

I have written this letter in my head so often yet I cannot think how to start it. So there it is . . . started! I am hesitant because I do not want to cause you any worry but just to say, hello. We had a dramatic encounter during the war and I sometimes think there is no reason why you should remember me but

I have probably thought of you every day since. During the Blitz in May 1941 I was driving an ambulance that was caught up in a severe bomb blast on St Anne's Road in Liverpool and you picked me up off the road and carried me into a building there. We lay together through that night and we separated when the all-clear went at dawn. I certainly believed we did not have long to live and I asked you to make love to me. I have a daughter, Agnes, a beautiful and clever child, who I think may be yours, however I want you to know that I have since married a good kind man who loves us both dearly. We are happy, the three of us, and he believes that he is her father as well he may be and this letter is not to ask you for anything. But I feel a great need to speak to you for I feel that as a result of that night, you are woven into my life in a way that I cannot deny and so I am writing to tell you a bit about myself.

There is a knock on the door, a traveller from Porlock no doubt.

No. It is Sally. 'Coffee, Prof?'

I hope to be allowed to die in this room for it has many comforts, spiritual comforts as well as practical ones. Officially I now have cardiovascular issues. From here I can hear the bells ring out the hours from St Ethelburga's, the same age as the university, and only a hop and a skip away. Not that I do much hopping these days but I can still get there without too much trouble. And I can see trees and the sky and the clouds; for a while I had belonged to the cloud appreciation society. Not for me just a little patch of blue. And the books. Everywhere on all the walls. My precious.

I stir the coffee and sip it. At breakfast we're given percolated coffee but at elevenses it is instant. Quite good though. I bite into the shortbread biscuit, brushing the crumbs onto the floor. 'Remorse of his Duty'. Yes, a good phrase. And a good meaning. Not obsolete for me.

I have chosen my burial plot. Not officially but secretly, dreamily. One day soon. But before I am free to die I must settle this affair and tomorrow I will give Agnes the letter that her mother had given me to deliver all those years ago. Was it more than fifty years ago? Almost a lifetime ago. Maybe I should have given it to Agnes long before this but always, all my life, I have been anxious not to disturb the flow of things. To do the steady thing. And, specifically, to look after the child. The loveliness of the child Agnes had undermined me and her unhappiness I had found intolerable. I justified inaction on the grounds that it had been imperative to look after her. To do the responsible thing. How tempting it could be to wade to the centre of the floor and wave one's arms about and shout about some extraordinary event so that everyone would turn and stare and say, in various states of unbelief, I can't believe that! I have always been a wallflower. Watching, waiting, preserving the peace, as I see it. A liminal creature, as I used to think of it. Now I can see I am just a coward.

On that dreadful day, when I had gone down to deliver the car and to collect Agnes, Sophy had whispered to me with that joyful smile on her face, 'I just want to meet him, Mally. I just want to meet him and see him. After all, he is part of my life now.'

My full name is Sophy Florence van der Berg but when we met I was Sophy Florence Miller. My father is a vicar in the Church of England and he would have liked you, I am sure. Maybe you would have liked him. Perhaps you will meet one day? He is very clever. He has a noble face and he looks both kind and wise. He can have rather a prim demeanour. I sometimes think he would have made a good monk since he is barely of this world. He would have shaken your hand with an immense courtesy while he leant towards you and smiled with his carefully closed mouth and his steady eyes would have examined you and found you wanting. He is, according to the fashion for men of the cloth, a freemason and a eugenicist and he sees in me a partial solution to the problem of womanhood. On his desk he has on the one side a bust of Plato and on the other Julius Caesar. I think he believes that Jesus Christ combines the virtues of both these heroes and probably spoke with the cadences of Shakespeare. My mother is a necessary facility since he truly believes it is 'marry or burn'. Sex is a nasty dirty thing that men need and women must tolerate. Children are their compensation. It may be hard to believe, then, that I really do love my father very much.

The loss of Sophy broke my father's heart so profoundly that although he continued to live, and to work, and to preach, and to minister, he never really saw anyone properly again. His height shrank. His soul shrank. My mother suffered terribly too and I found it hard to talk to them at all.

And of course I love my mother very much too but she is harder to love, keeping me at a distance. My father hugs me often, my mother never. I, and my younger brother Malcolm, are the confused and confusing marriage of these two.

Were we confused? We were certainly very eager to do the right thing at all times. I still am. What were the reasons for my hesitation in handing the letter over to Joe? Agnes's small world had been shattered by the loss of her parents. This was no time for new people. My parents were far from ideal but at least Agnes knew them, and they loved her very profoundly in their own way. She would always have a home with them where I could see her and keep an eye on things. We represented continuity, such as it was. It seemed irresponsible to bring Joe into the picture at that time. I had no idea what kind of man he was. So, I put the letter away. In addition, the pedant in me argued that there are many ways to tell a story and this letter was no more than the romantic outpouring of Sophy's possibly transient feelings. She was a young woman suffused with passion for a chap encountered at a time of maximum danger with all the customary concomitant emotions aroused during intense wartime experiences. Why then didn't I just burn it? Well, that has always been a strange thing about me. I store things. Even very painful memories. Looking back now, I have collected notes of rejection from lovers, God knows, enough, but I treasure them as I treasure the love letters. All part of my history. So the letter went in with that lot, not that there were many when I was only twenty. And you could argue that it was not mine to burn. However, I did do one further thing at that stage. I opened it and read it.

Reading it again now, I am reminded and even surprised by how much she talked about Kurt, her husband, his Dutch father, Willem, his German mother Agnes and their life in Rotterdam. After Agnes was killed in the Allied bombing over there at the beginning of the war Willem and Kurt managed to get to England and were interned for a while. It was my father's insistence on inviting refugees to lunch that meant we met them both. Sophy went into a lot of details about her marriage to Kurt and how safe she felt with him.

> He is artistic, funny, very physical. He has large beautiful hands with wide well-shaped palms and long fingers. He sketches in the air when he talks for he thinks in pictures.

I could not see why she provided so much detail about him but I suspect it was Sophy's way of exorcising any potential deceitfulness. She had decided to love Kurt and make a life with him and she wanted to be free to do so despite that fact that, plainly, Joe had won her heart. At the time that she married she had no way of knowing whether Joe would ever return from the war; his life would have been at risk every hour. She needed a father for her baby and Kurt was devoted to her and, in time, devoted to both of them. There was a pragmatic side to my sister. And, the truth is, she had no way then of knowing who her baby's father was.

She thought the world of Willem who eulogised Spinoza. Sophy had an extraordinary capacity to see wonder and goodness in people that I regarded as rather ordinary. 'All her geese are swans,' my mother used to complain as we met yet another of Sophy's 'wonderful' people. Nonetheless, Willem was an appealing character, that was true. He and Kurt had retained a sort of romantic innocence despite everything. It could be intensely irritating at times; a blind refusal to face facts, my father said and I agreed with him.

> After a few glasses of beer he always quotes Spinoza on the subject of free will which Spinoza (and I quote) placed not in free decision but in free necessity. 'We are all impelled by external causes and, in addition, we operate according to our own necessity', he said. He talked about a stone that had been thrown, saying that the stone, while being impelled by an external cause, if it were conscious would imagine that it is in charge of its own motion, and he used this example to illustrate that men are conscious of their own desires but are ignorant of the origins of these desires. By this time the room would be full of cigarette smoke and we would all be swilling beer; he is a marvellous person.
>
> I have often wondered, Joe, what causes impelled us together that night. I remember it all so vividly. The roar of the bombs and the planes reaching us as though from another universe. Some moonlight filtering through the dust falling onto the floor through the empty window frames although I

could barely see your face. At one stage I remember holding it away from me and staring up at the outline of your head. Did you say something? I wasn't sure. 'Love me,' I begged. 'Love me, please.' And, Joe, you would have thought we had all the time in the world and perhaps we did for when you are completely unafraid of dying, time loses its meaning. As the world crashed around us, the AA guns going, the landmines falling and the enormous blasts shaking the walls of our refuge we lay there, at one, at peace. Do you remember that we were whispering although the whole area was full of the sound of the screeching air raid warnings? Sometimes I look back and think that that night with its threat of imminent death, and the warmth of your body and its powerful bond with mine, represented the closest I have ever been to anyone in my whole life.

When the all-clear finally went it was nearly dawn and, as we left our sanctuary, I could see that your hair was grey with dust. I remember we kissed one more time and then I watched you running through the rubble towards the docks and I limped back to the ambulance station. I never did find the other shoe. The damage was tremendous. I walked down roads past the fronts of houses which were all that remained of former homes. One had a cat sitting sadly on the front step. Survivors were dragging at the fallen timbers hoping to recover children, parents, everything that they had lost. I had to ask myself why we had survived.

When I got back to Merebridge my parents were both out but my brother Malcolm was there. He was only fifteen. As we grew up together, we felt like conspirators against the world: if anyone threatened either of us the other would come to the rescue. That included, occasionally, our parents. He is a thin, anxious boy. He sleeps badly. He is bullied at school. Of course, there is nothing I can do about that but I talk to him about life, as it were, trying to give him some ideas to fall back on. As I opened the back door he was sitting at the kitchen table and he looked up at me with one of his astonishing smiles and got up and walked rapidly across the room, grasping me by the shoulders while he examined my face with great care.

It was curious to read this about myself all those years ago and still strange now. How well she loved me and wanted to look after me. I was not then yet a toad, I was tall and skinny, a callow youth, an observer might have said. My preoccupations much what they are now: the chance of sex, joys of drink, the escape offered by books. Had I been bullied? No more than any swotty kid. I could remember her walking in through the kitchen door, covered in dust, dirty and with her clothes torn and only one shoe. She had a graze on one cheek. She looked like the survivor of a bomb blast that she was. However, I soon realised that she had been shaken by a much more significant event. I think I told her the cathedral had been destroyed and offered her some tea. I expected her to be shocked and horrified but she was bubbling with excitement.

'Mally, I have just had the most extraordinary night. I can hardly believe it myself. I met this chap, a young doctor, he has gone to sign up today, and we made love on a bench, in a hall, somewhere off St Anne's Road.'

Of course, I found it hard to credit and I questioned her closely. He was a newly qualified doctor and he was joining his regiment that day and they had spent the night together during the bombing raid and it was wonderful. I immediately suspected the chap of taking advantage of her but she insisted, no, he was a perfect gentleman. It had been the best night of her life. I wondered about pregnancy and she reluctantly agreed, yes, a worry. She had been so intoxicated by the experience that I could see it would take her a while to come down to earth.

'Who is he?'

'His name is Joe. Dr Joseph Bradshaw.'

I thought often of you, out there with your regiment in the desert. I wondered what it would be like to be in danger every day of your life in an unfamiliar place, to be moving every week, to be unsure about your next meal, your next drink of water, to watch people die in agony, to try to save them with limited medical resources and to fail sometimes. To be always tired, always anxious, always alert. To stare day after day over the unforgiving desert sands in the sun and the heat. I wondered whether you had been killed and had to accept that I would not know. But I promised myself that if we both survived the war, I would ask you if we could meet, just so that I could see your face, look into your eyes, find out what colour your hair is. You had said you would not have to shoot anyone: your job would be to patch people up. I read the news reports of the war in the desert: I read of Rommel, Montgomery, the tanks and the desert rats. I hoped nobody shot at you.

However, something was changing. The birth of Agnes meant that you were now visibly and actually with me every day. I felt in every cell of my body that I was being unfaithful to my child's true father. One day I confided in Malcolm. Endearingly, he offered a sociological perspective.

'We are war babies, Sophy. We grew up with so much uncertainty, so much fear, so much sense that life was just a brief strut upon the stage' (he was my father's son, after all) 'that lasting, durable emotions are pointless, easily shattered, easily lost. Now, we find we are still alive and the bombs are gone and the skies are clear and we have these structures we built for ourselves during times of danger and now we find we don't need them any more and they are prisons not refuges and we want to leave. We have learned to live with the provisional and now we find we cannot live with the permanent.'

And I could remember this quite vividly. Sophy had asked me to go for a walk with her while our mother was looking after Agnes and as soon as we were away from the house she had told me how conflicted she felt. 'Tormented' was the word she used.

I wonder what you are thinking, Joe, if you are still reading. I feel as though I have written a book.

Meanwhile, I know you would love Agnes. She is so bright, so quick. She is such a good reader already and loves books. As she grows older I can see she is so brave, setting herself such high standards, that she loves me so fiercely. Please God, I pray to the God I do for that moment believe in, don't let me do anything to destroy her hopes, her faith in the chance that life might be good, to hurt or harm her. For she loves Kurt too; and I had such a craving for the feeling of you in my arms again and your hands on my skin that sometimes it seemed I would go mad, trying to return to that long-distanced, no doubt idealised, moment. Reason could not defeat this longing. And so, we carry on, me and my perfect family.

I have tracked Father O'Connor down, Joe, and he invited me into the presbytery and said he could get a letter to you. I saw a flight of stairs and those must be the stairs where you had sat as a little boy.

I left with his blessing, an invisible dog barking, sad that I had not been able to climb the stairs and see the bedroom you had slept in. But my heart was singing. You were alive. And I could contact you. I could write and introduce myself and then maybe we could meet. We would meet. I was quite confident about that. Yes, my heart was singing and that night I was able to take Kurt into my arms with renewed love, not passion, but compassion. I wanted to love him in a way that made him happy. And I knew I could. The clouds lifted and the skies cleared and I was joyful again.

And this is the letter, Joe. As you can tell, I have poured my heart into it. No-one knows as much about me as you do now. I hope I have not frightened you away. I will give it to Malcolm to deliver. If I never hear anything I will not do anything more. It seemed important to write this and when I have time I will try to work out why.

Thank you for reading this far, Joe. Look after yourself and if you can bring yourself to respond I will be so happy to hear from you. I cannot end without confessing, I love you.

Sophy

I slowly replaced the letter in the envelope. It was heartbreaking, really. In person, Sophy could give the impression of being cold. Cerebral, people called her. I believed that that was why she had been so drawn to Kurt and why he was so good for her. He had been warm. Not just hot-blooded, he was in every way larger than life. He exuded warmth and kindliness and safety and I think, for all her theorising, that is what drew my sister to him. But, clearly she had already given her heart to Joe.

When I had gone down to deliver the car she had told me how happy the three of them had been. 'Last night we sat out on our little porch, Mally. Sensational views over to the horizon as the sun went down, the sky was yellow and the sea and even all the puddles of seawater lying on the sands. It was amazing, Mally. I wish you had seen it.' I didn't think I had ever seen her so sparkly and happy, and indiscreet. I felt envious of her abundant and overflowing happiness. 'And, we are trying for another baby, Mally. You are going to be an uncle again!'

And then, the dreadful aftermath. Our father buried her beside her husband in the churchyard. He was never the same man again. Our mother remained tight-lipped throughout and for years after that she stayed at home on Sundays, with Agnes and me when I was there, refusing to go to my father's church. And I got used to being the only child of this ill-matched couple. I think I had always known that Sophy was their love-child for by the time I was born their love for each other had more or less run out. They loved me a lot but it was, according to the *mores* of the home, a dutiful love. Sophy was their ewe-lamb, their promise for the future, their favourite and their first-born. And if there was another love-child, it was Agnes.

I forgot about the letter. Perhaps I chose to forget about it. But if I did think about it it was usually with a degree of satisfaction; I was fairly confident I had done the right thing.

Agnes grew up to be as clever as anything and went off to university. There were a lot of admirers, some of whom I met, but she chose none of the university chaps. Richard was a stockbroker, very wealthy, very 'clubbable' which should have been a warning. A mild-mannered man. Beware of them. I liked him well enough but I was surprised. I think Agnes had decided to do what looked like the safe thing. She wanted security. She had a mercenary side, possibly due to living with two old grandparents with very little money. Soon she was pregnant. She lost the baby and she left Richard for a while and went to stay with Moira, a university friend. One day when I was visiting them, Agnes told me that she was in therapy with a wonderful therapist that Charles had found for her, Charles being the family GP and a long-standing friend of Richard's. 'Dr Bradshaw, Mally. Joe Bradshaw.' I was horrified. What were the chances of that? Apparently Charles's father was Joe's best friend and senior colleague. But at that stage I felt I could say nothing. Agnes was settled, she said it was doing her so much good, finally processing the deaths of her parents. She did not stay in therapy for long. She returned to Richard and a bit later Elfie was born.

Years later I was invited to Elfie's seventh birthday party, cake for the kiddies and champagne for the grown-ups. By that time Richard and Agnes had divorced and Richard had married Bettina. No-one had a bad word to say about Bettina and in my experience, normally when this happens, one is talking about some anodyne, empty personality towards whom neither love nor hate can be felt. Bettina was young, with a tennis-player's limber body and a wide smile showing perfect teeth; it would have been easy to dislike her but she never gave grounds for that.

While I was there I was propped up against the counter in the kitchen while Bettina was finalising the decorations on the cake alongside the seven candles when I said, tentatively, 'I hear Agnes went to a really good therapist when she and Richard first split up. Someone Charles found. She seems so well and happy now.'

'Oh God,' said Bettina. 'Please don't say anything to Agnes, or Charles for that matter, but my sister, Molly, is heavily involved with him.'

'Involved?'

'Very much involved. As in having a massive love affair and

he is going to marriage counselling with his wife and wants to leave her and Molly is in pieces. She is crazy about him. He is an absolute Don Juan in my opinion and he may be an amazing therapist but God forbid he should have anything more to do with Agnes.'

As I drove home I thanked God I had never delivered the letter.

So, what had happened in the intervening years that made me change my mind? A conversation I had with Joe himself, six months ago. I was back at Lippington House for a New Year's Eve party. This was a rare occasion and I think Richard and Bettina had asked everyone they knew. Agnes was not there. She had gone to spend Xmas in Newfoundland with Theo's parents. Theo was Elfie's boyfriend and there were rumours of a wedding one day soon. He was an intern at Lloyd's and a very good-looking boy who was said to have been spotted by Richard who then introduced him to Elfie. Richard as matchmaker; an interesting concept. I felt sure Bettina had played a part but when I questioned her she would only say, 'You have to meet him, Malcolm, and then make up your own mind. But, yes, I like him very much.'

When I got to Lippington, Bettina introduced me to a tall, well-preserved woman saying, 'Malcolm, meet my older sister Molly.' Aha, I thought, so this is Molly! She told me her partner,

Conrad, was there. I asked her if he was Joe Bradshaw to most people and certainly when he was practising as a therapist. She agreed and said they had been together now for many years. So, he has settled down, I said to myself. We moved on and drifted around. Charles and I chatted about this and that. He asked me how Agnes was and I was able to say that Oriel College was treating her well and she was both enjoying and complaining about the extra tutorial hours she had recently been offered. Also, long-distance planning the wedding for Elfie. As the witching hour approached I wandered out onto the terrace. It was a cold night and I had collected my coat and sat happily on one of the old benches positioned so they have their backs to the abundance of gorgeous creepers that cover the house walls, looking out onto the panorama of the garden. And it was a panorama. A slight frost from a few nights ago had lingered in the shadows of this secret and mantled place and the branches of the trees were glistening in the light of an almost full moon. I had brought with me a tumbler of malt and sat there, as one does on such an occasion, feeling full of love for humanity. Then I heard a voice. ‘May I join you? We haven’t met. I am Joe Bradshaw.’

We shook hands and I introduced myself while I examined him with interest. At this stage Joe Bradshaw was just around eighty, still rather distinguished looking, and I felt a pang of envy when I reflected that he was a decade older than I was. He had a naturally graceful body and a voice that resonated with the timbre of a fine tenor. His features were strong and regular and he had an impressively high forehead. And he struck me as being possessed of an abundance of resources. What I mean by that is that he seemed to me to be good-looking, clever, successful, even lucky, as well as prosperous. He was the opposite of needy in every respect. Instinctively, l felt I could trust him but that made me wary; such an attribute is often the necessary garb of the conman. Bearing in mind what I knew of his past, I decided to let him talk and see where it got us.

He had gone as far as bringing a decanter with him which he placed on a table nearby as he sat down next to me. He was plainly quite inebriated. So was I, but Joe was even further down the road. I have always maintained that a man who is able to be a calm and cheerful drunk is at base a good man. And Joe turned out to be one of those. We shared a few pleasantries and sipped side by side in a companionable manner.

'I was glad to meet Molly,' I ventured. 'She seems very nice.'

'Yes, to my surprise, quite frankly, we are still together. Nearly twenty years. I think we are still happy.'

Just as I was beginning to believe I had perhaps misjudged the man, he began to talk about Agnes. 'Charles has just told me that you are the Malcolm who is Agnes's uncle? So I guess you know she was once my patient, a long time ago.'

Charles, I thought, incorrigibly indiscreet.

'Of course, patient confidentiality and all that but she had a great effect on me. There are always patients who get under one's skin, in a manner of speaking, and Agnes did that. I remember the first time I saw her. Always significant, I think. It was my mother's birthday and I remember staring at myself in the mirror that morning, thinking about her – my mother I mean – while I was shaving and thinking how old I looked and how corrupt. Sin has always weighed heavily with me and I had been no saint: Catholic upbringing, you see. Never leaves you. I was beginning to find virtue tempting. And the doublethink at the heart of psychoanalysis was beginning to tire me: the idea that one deserves to be the confessor and the other, the sinner, the confessee or is it the confessant? No-one ever told me anything that was half as startling as my own sins, if that is what they were. And then, in she walked. Not then, of course, later that day. She was very young but then there always were a lot of young women around me. At work, you know. Trainees and so on. She had a quality of distance, an aloofness, as though no matter how close one got to her she would always be a bit out of reach. I indicated that she should sit in the armchair at an angle to my own. "We need to introduce ourselves," I said. "The couch comes later." And even as I said it I could sense something seedy in my voice, as though it were to be the casting couch. Ludicrous, but this is what I felt. I could say, this is what she did to me. She sat down and crossed her very beautiful legs and I carried out the assessment. In some ways, nothing new. The human face has a limited number of features and so does a human life. Love, hate, fear, grief, joy, hope. The distinctions between people emerge in our responses to these events. The grief was consuming but she told her story well. This was our unlived life, in a manner of speaking. A young mother and lost beloved infant son, in her case a late miscarriage, and I knew that, if he had lived, he would have been a happy child, like me. And then, she recounted what I call the vision and eventually I concluded that this was the shaping event; the paradigm of her sense of incompleteness. She became preoccupied by a memory of her parents the day they died. I suppose that would have been your sister and brother-in-law? She had collected her mother's cigarettes from the porch of the place where they were staying and she ran in with them and felt that she had startled them, maybe in the middle of an embrace. She said they were only partly clothed and they had their arms around each other and her mother's hair was tousled and she was shining, that is the word she used, shining with joy. For her it was a vision, for she used that word, of what love was. And she explained that she had never yet found it and, imagine me, I am sitting there wondering whether I have ever found it either.'

He stopped and looked at me, a bit blearily, while pouring a bit more into our tumblers. 'Why is it always the second or third drink that just tastes the best? Or is it the fourth or fifth? I'm afraid I have lost count. You are a good listener, Malcolm. But I am sure I am telling you nothing you don't already know.'

And I was remembering Sophy as she had been when I went down the coast to hand over the car. Her joy, her delight, her happiness.

'You don't need to go on,' I said, anxious that he should not feel compromised although I was desperate to learn more.

'It was years ago,' he said. 'Years. And you are her uncle. I just want to say that I behaved throughout with the utmost professionalism but more than that I was scrupulous and virtuous. In order to ensure I stayed within the right boundaries I told my best friend, Benny. I told my agent. I even told another young woman, my senior registrar at the time. That was reckless. Of course, the clichés came back at me. "You must talk about it," she said. "Don't let it fester." I must have looked unimpressed by this advice. "If you can't talk about it, write it down. That sometimes helps. You must get it outside of yourself." But that was the last thing I wanted, Malcolm. I wanted to keep it inside. All of it. I wanted to be filled with it, saturated with this sense of urgency, obsession, desire. I did not want to lose an ounce of this precious stuff, whatever it was, which I could almost see dribbling through my fingers while I stared in horror at my cupped palms, desperate to save every drop of this life-saving elixir. And I knew it well. I had sipped it before. Gulped it, in fact. Often. But never like this. This, I told myself, was different.' He was talking to himself by now, as he stared at his hands held out as though for alms, but at that point he stopped and looked up at me. 'You know what I mean, don't you, Malcolm?'

'So you were in love with her?' I said.

'It does happen,' he said quite sharply. 'It is not that uncommon. Analyst in love with patient. It only matters when the analyst loses control and I did not.'

He lit another cigarette and offered me one. I had learned that he was an inveterate smoker. 'She went back to him, that is what I never understood. To Richard. Our host. He seems a decent enough guy and you must know him better than I do but I thought maybe it meant she was not incorruptible after all. I decided after much thought that it must be the garden. This garden. This little bit of heaven. She was certainly in love with this,' and he waved his hand with the cigarette in it out towards the shimmering grass whitened by moonlight. 'She was not, you know, a gardener. It was the one aspect of her wealth that truly thrilled her: access to this little bit of heaven with a million ardent attendants to keep it this way.'

And then he changed tack again. 'You see, it really is about internal resonances. She and I had echoes of similar losses: our mothers when we were very young. Too young. Too young to know that this was an extraordinary tragedy that would mark us forever.'

And as I listened to his musical voice describing the nature of his love for Agnes I very nearly said, 'I have a letter for you from her mother,' but I did not. It is never good to make decisive gestures when drunk and on a whim.

We talked a bit more, discussed the garden for a while, the weather, heaven knows what else, we were both quite the worse for wear by then. And then Molly appeared and took him off, having given me a disapproving look. In honour of my family connections I had been given a bedroom upstairs. I drove home the next day, hungover and full of thought.

Since then, as the months have passed and news of Elfie's wedding this summer has been spreading through the family I have become increasingly sure that the time has come to deliver the letter. However, having delayed for so long, having in truth believed that the the path of virtue was to withhold a letter that could scarcely, on account of its momentous contents, avoid spreading consternation, I find myself burdened now by a fear of delivering it too late; its harm related more to the timing than the contents. If Joe is all he now seems to me to be, he should have had this letter a long time ago and offering it to Agnes, (not

Joe) at the wedding reception may be a further act of cowardice, hoping to conceal my bad faith amidst the crowding distractions of a family get-together. However, at least both Joe and Agnes will be there so I could, I think, reasonably expect Agnes to show it to Joe or even to pass it on. Under the circumstances, I feel confident this is the right way to do things although now and again I feel a ripple of unease in case I am about to shake things up too much. Joe can certainly become very emotional and God knows I would not want to upset Agnes, particularly on her daughter's wedding day, however I think this is probably a good time to act. She has never remarried and it is about time she had a prosperous father-figure to depend on. After all these years, with everyone concerned grown up, and the war really just a memory for the oldies, I expect any emotions left over from the past will be more manageable. And I do feel the need to own up to my cowardice as far as little Agnes is concerned although I think since then most people would say I have acted reasonably honourably. The Enlightenment values I grew up with, reason and order, seem to me to have prevailed in the end. So if it seems the time is ripe, Agnes will have the letter at the reception.

The patient is obliged to repeat the repressed material as a contemporary experience instead of, as the physician would prefer to see, remembering it as something belonging to the past.

Beyond the Pleasure Principle, Sigmund Freud

DR JOSEPH CONRAD BRADSHAW

The day before the Wedding Reception

PROFESSOR FREUD, THAT CUNNING Viennese magician, is shunned and devalued now, but in his time he certainly knew a thing or two and one thing he knew well is that it is not so easy to keep the past back there where it belongs since it tends to leak into the present all the time. No matter how firmly you slam the watertight door and lock it and then throw the whole weight of your body against it in order to resist the monstrous pressure exerted on the other side by all those emotions from the past which you do not want to feel again, you will fail and they will smash through and hurl you to the ground and then once more overwhelm you. This is my most recent example: just now, while pouring out our breakfast coffee, Molly told me that the invitation to go down to her sister's big house in Lippington tomorrow, which has been in the calendar for months, is to attend a wedding reception for Elfie, Bettina's stepdaughter. Immediately the knowledge that this will almost certainly mean Agnes will be there has made my old heart contract with joy.

I have, in a sense, been waiting for this (I'm tempted to say, waiting all my life but of course that is nonsense); however, I have known for a long time that since she and I are now members of the same extended family it was probable, but I could never be sure when, or even if we would meet again. And both professional and personal pride forbade me from ever trying to engineer it. But wedding celebrations involve whole families and so now, fate has dropped this gift into my hands and at once, as I stirred my coffee with 'a studied calm', all the old feelings surged back. Cynics would say, time will have weathered my awkward passions, age will have dulled both of us. However, I doubt they will have had any effect at all, for what she was she still will be. And, sitting here now, I know that outwardly altered though I am, I remain the same. What will Agnes see? An old man but although my hair is white now, it is still plentiful, and I am mobile, reasonably agile, and certainly effortlessly articulate. Genetics is an unfair lottery but at least in these respects I have been a winner and mirrors have always been my friends; it was the internal reflections of which I was so afraid, which

I turned away from with a resigned shrug of dismay. For who would want to see what I saw there? So I can still wear a suit well but this morning in the bathroom mirror my eyes shifted even under my own scrutiny.

When I think of Agnes during her hours of therapy, what I recall most vividly are the remembrances she brought to mind of my young mother. Images of her began to leak into the life I then shared with Agnes during those hours when she lay on the couch in my consulting room, watching the tops of the beech trees in the garden below quartered by the sunlit window panes. As I listened to her voice I used to see the squares of sunlight move from beside my desk to the foot of the couch. Logic tells me it could not always have been there but memory tells me differently. And that would then transport me even further back over the years to my life as a child with my mother. Imagine a young girl over from Ireland to Liverpool, a Catholic girl, who had found work in service at a big house on the west coast of England. She is pregnant and it is me. Could I have been *in situ* when she arrived? I knew nothing of all this as six-year-olds in general do not know more than what they see. I knew I was happy. I was well fed, I was warm, I was loved and I was good, for why would I be otherwise? Until that day when I stood in those squares of sunlight on the landing as I watched a stranger carrying blood-stained sheets out of my mother's bedroom.

That night there were unfamiliar footsteps in the house, urgent whispered conversations outside the door and someone came in to tell me that my mother had gone.

'Gone where?' I asked, bewildered, for I knew she would never leave me behind.

I seem to recall standing by the open window of my attic bedroom, staring out at the wide empty stretch of the sea. A breeze was bouncing off it and bringing from over the links the scent of the sand and grass to me. I thought of my memories and I wound words around them and tucked them safely away in my mind for I knew I would need them one day. I think even then I realised that they might enable me to survive.

When I think of my mother I can see a distant pale face and an aureole of hair as she stands at the top of a flight of stairs calling to me with an infinite tenderness. I struggle up the stairs, enormous as they are, examining the patterns on the carpet as I go, my small hands leading me up and up and there, on a level with my eyes, are her lovely, sandalled feet as she bends down with youthful suppleness and strength and lifts me up above her head. My special clever boy, she says. My darling boy.

But there is another memory, more important, not long, I think, before she dies. She lifts the sheet and slides into my bed beside me. She is soft and warm through her cold nightdress. 'I am so cold,' she says. I put my arms around her neck and she wraps her arms around my body, hugging me to absorb my warmth. Her face is wet against mine and her dark hair soft and springy in my hands. I taste salt when I kiss her cheeks. I can sense how my small body warms her and consoles her. Her soft breasts cushion me and my legs are curled against her stomach. Her breath brushes my face. The softness beneath the thin cotton, the overwhelming sense of her hair, her skin, even her bones beneath the skin. My small heart swells to a vast size; it grows as large as the world so as to encompass she who is my world. This was my memory and I had words to wrap it in. And so I believed, even at six, as I stared out of the window into the future that I would survive.

After she had died I was thrown on the mercy of the parish, which responded magnificently. I was taken in and housed, loved, lectured, well fed and well educated by Father Michael O'Connor, of whose church my mother had been a loyal member. Those were innocent days. He was a small, smiling priest from County Mayo with a taste for whisky and a fund of salacious jokes about monks and priests and housekeepers which I did not understand until much later. I heard most of them too young, sitting snugly on the stairs as the Squire and Father Michael shared a dram. The Squire, I think, could have been another candidate. He too was generous, paying for my school uniform, inviting me back to the big house for games of chess, and funding my life as a student when I had made my way via grammar school to the University of Liverpool Medical School. I like to think of my mother as someone who might have loved both these disparate men in ways that fulfilled their lives a little more. And hers too. They must have been fond of her. They could not have been kinder to me had either been the father I often speculated about.

So, what has this to do with my patient still, as it were, lying patiently on the couch before me, the sunlight still resting there on the floor, quiescent like some sort of magic carpet? She too was an orphan. Her parents had died in a car accident after the war. The point is that, while my visual recollection of my mother is hazy, the moment my patient first entered my consulting room I could see in her shape, in her posture, in her face, in her movements, all the gratifying lineaments of my lost mother. Not to put too fine a point on it, she was terrifyingly familiar. I very nearly lost control and burst into tears. And then, every week the impression intensified until sometime later, as she was lying there on the couch, a foot or two away from me, the distant beech trees waving in a fine summer wind and me tremulous with the return of repressed sensations, she crying, desperate, panicky, telling me I was her last hope of sanity, me swamped by the memories of my mother holding me in her arms that night, all those concomitant sensory impingements insisting, persisting in threading their way through every word that fell from her mouth, I realised for the first time how god-like I had felt all those years ago. What power I had, what potency. I found myself back there, wondrously gratified by being able to console, to warm and revivify the person I loved most in all the world. And it was into this emotional context that Agnes had walked on her first session and I believe I have been trying to negotiate my way out of it ever since.

So this is the source of my osmotic love for this young woman. I thought at first the true origin of her distress was loss. Having lost her parents so young, she, like me, was saturated with a vast and ineradicable sense of what might have been. And the precipitating event that had brought her to me: the loss of a baby. She had felt the quickening. She had dreamt the dreams. When the infant was in its second trimester, she miscarried. The blood, the pain, the hospital, the horror. Worst of all, she believed that her husband had been instrumental in the baby's death. He had pushed her, she thought by accident, while she was standing at the top of a small flight of steps from the kitchen to the garden. She had fallen, heavily, and he had then tried to help her up, appalled, I suspect, at what he might have done. She miscarried a week later. No-one could prove anything but my patient had felt shamed by it as well as wounded. It was the abiding grief mingled with fear that had driven her to my couch.

Briefly into my mind came a sense of what it would have been like to have her as my mother. How fortunate her son would have been for I could tell that the quality of her love would have been exceptional. I could tell he would have bathed himself in that love and have been a happy child like me. And then, she recounted the 'vision' and eventually I concluded that this was the shaping event; the paradigm of her sense of incompleteness. She became preoccupied by a memory of her parents the day they died, of her dark-haired mother and her blond father, as she described it, standing close together, loving each other and loving her as she runs into the room with their cigarettes.

I tried going further back and saw only later how significant this little conversation was. The 'vision' preceded by merely a few hours the ultimate horror of her life. When I led her back there, carefully, hesitantly, she remembered nothing although she had been told that her mother's younger brother Malcolm had taken her back to Merebridge where her grandparents lived.

'By car?'

'No, he had left his car with my father. That was what killed them. My mother used to drive ambulances but it was assumed that my dad would drive them. Sexual politics of the time.'

'So, by train?'

'Apparently. I have no recollection of the journey at all but he brought me to my grandparents' home and in the morning when I woke up they told me that my parents were dead.'

'Do you remember who told you?'

'No, might have been my uncle or either of my grandparents.'

I could not see her face clearly but her voice was painfully sad.

'Do you remember anything of that time?'

'I remember at some stage being taken down to the promenade for a walk. It is what people did at that time. When you were at a loose end. And looking at the horizon and the line of water that represented the sea and wondering if my parents were there. I mean, where do people go? To a child it is impossible for a parent, a mother or a father, to just not exist. I decided they were elsewhere and that I just had to get used to that. Merely out of sight. I had to get used to loving people whom I could not see, at a distance, beyond the horizon.'

'Quite a thought for a little girl such as you were.'

And she had smiled a little at that, turning her head a bit, 'Am I being a bit precocious? Maybe it wasn't really as clearly formulated then.'

'Or maybe it was,' I had said.

As the months passed, and the sessions continued, it seemed that her memories became my memories and I could no longer remember which were her memories and which were mine since her memories were always clothed with mine. What did I know of her experience of love or hope or loss or longing or trees or sunlight for that matter except by reference to my own knowledge of these things? Or, indeed, of warmth or desire, of softness or skin or hair?

And I had, of course, told Clara about her; Clara my then live-in girlfriend, as I preferred to refer to her, 'partner' being so pompous. She is a medic and a paediatrician. She sees too much of children, she used to say, and as a result she had no wish to have her own, which is a great relief. She put down her knitting, which she works at because she says it relieves her of stress, and gave me what I can only describe as an old-fashioned look.

'Oh my God. Have you done anything?'

'What? Why does everyone ask me that? What would I do? No, of course not. Anyway, she is leaving soon.'

She picked up her knitting again. She was born in the Faroe Islands, where as far as I can tell, everyone knits, and manages to be both statuesque and svelte in the way only the Scandinavians can manage. She grew up in Copenhagen and has reddish-blonde hair and is very bright and very sexy and I used to daily expect her to leave me.

'It would be the end of everything, you know that, don't you?'

I was not sure whether she meant the end of our relationship, the end of my career or the end of my life and I did not ask. Maybe all three.

'She only has another couple of weeks. She has actually done rather well.'

'You're not having a breakdown, are you?'

'Of course not. Just a lot to handle right now.'

My patient's last session was textbook stuff. She arrived on time and left on time. No-one cried. No-one brought presents. I could see that she was now robust enough to stand alone. Like me, she had made her peace with grief and her husband could no longer undermine her wellbeing. It was a neat, clean termination to a short successful analysis and I believed Sigmund would have been proud of it. Naturally, my heart was breaking. But, as it happened, it was not yet the end of the story.

A few weeks later I went for a haircut to my favourite place near the centre of the city. I was early, as usual, and popped into the little cafe next door for my customary coffee. I always order the mocha and it was usually rather good. As I walked in, I saw Agnes sitting at a table for two, the seat next to her empty. She immediately looked confused and embarrassed but emboldened maybe by my involuntary smile (no longer securely constrained within the boundaries of psychoanalytic practice I could not help myself) she smiled back and gestured towards the empty seat. So I sat down next to her.

'Hello,' she said, shyly.

'Hello.' I was trying to retrieve my dignity but secretly felt overwhelmed with delight in encountering her in this way. She looked wonderful. I had only seen her face within the restricted light of my consulting room and here the untrammelled sunlight glowed about her and glinted off her skin.

'I'm waiting for him.' She held out her hand. 'We are getting back together.' On the third finger shone a glossy colossal stone. 'It's an emerald,' she said with a smile, as though that explained everything.

I stared at it in horror for I was devastated. My goal had been to free her of her appetite for this Richard, this charming psychopath, as I had him labelled. But now I had to be careful. I knew I was staring at her. How beautiful women become when they are loved. And I watched her mouth. I had never been able to do that. How cleverly it shaped the words; how bright they were as they fell from her lips. I wanted to reach out and catch one and indeed I may even have tried to do so for I found my hand clasped by hers and moved to her cheek before she lifted it away and kissed the back of it.

But then I realised that she was waiting for my response, and I dragged some dusty old words out of my head.

'Congratulations, my dear. I hope you will be very happy.'

'Thank you,' she said. 'Thank you, Dr Bradshaw. Thank

you, Joe.' Her eyes were big with tears. I drew our clasped hands back towards my face and, opening her hand with mine, I kissed its palm and folded her fingers over it.

'Be happy, my dear Agnes,' I said, in my most avuncular tone. 'Be happy. Goodbye.'

But Clara was right, in a way. It was the beginning of the end of everything. Throughout my life, my adult life, at least, as a drunk lines up his drinks on the bar so I had lined up the affairs which would always, for a while at least, ease the pain. What pain? My mother's death, of course. Looking back down the years I see a litany of women, ever diminished by distance, like the perspective a hall of mirrors in a funfair offers the unwary punter; you go in for a few laughs and to smile at your distorted figure but all at once you step between two opposing mirrors and you have an unwanted glimpse of infinity. And there, tiny in the distance, at the end or is it the beginning of the long corridor of my memories, is the woman I call my mother. When I look back on all those intervening women and all those tempestuous beddings, I cannot help but see, as though a malevolent hand had switched on a giant X-ray machine, gleaming through the current knot of tangled limbs, the simplicity of that first unforgettable embrace in all its glory and triumph. I don't mean to be opaque. I am talking about my mother and myself. My first erotic experience. My formative erotic memory. Not, you understand, to be construed in terms of erections and penetrations and all the meat-factory business of actual sex but sex distilled. I knew something I had not known before about my own power to touch, to hold, to console and to satisfy, and I have searched for it in the arms of many women ever since. It is something of a talisman for me: what it represents is a touchstone for the value of my life, that once I was good and once I was loved.

Looking back, my work with Agnes dislodged me from this pattern, from what I had thought was to be my life's path, from my acceptance that this was to be the pattern of my life. That intimate if oblique reconnection with my mother transformed me, in other words. I had failed my patient but she had altered my life forever. I believe Spinoza said something to the effect that, if a stone that had been projected through the air had consciousness, it would believe it was moving of its own volition. If I felt as though I was making choices in the following years maybe I was simply following the trajectory that my encounter with Agnes had set me on.

Part two of this shameful story, some years later. Clara, by then, unwisely, my wife, was keynote lecturer at some conference and that evening I was doing my duty as escort. The educational setting where we met was a formidably large glass and concrete building, all sharp corners and big spaces filled with lighting which had clearly been forcibly subdued. Sounds, too, seem to fold themselves away with a discreet and apologetic air. Scents, odours found no place here; nothing seemed to breathe within these cold, smooth surfaces and precise angles. Clara was collecting an award of some sort and I did not want to seem disaffected but I found myself drifting to the edge of the gathering, looking down into a glass-lined quad where a swollen almost-blooming cactus stood marooned among concentric circles of uniform pebbles. While peering into this scene of desolation, I suddenly heard a voice say, 'Molly. My name is Molly,' and I turned towards it.

'Molly. That's my mother's name,' I said, involuntarily. Before me stood a group of men, maybe three or four, and among them was the woman who had spoken. Nondescript men, stuffed shirts, the uniform pebbles of our human race, while there between them stood this soft-petalled flower of a woman. She looked at me kindly. I cannot be alone in believing, every time I fall in love, that I am finally gazing at the features of the woman destined to be mine forever. Is this not the way it works?

She leant towards me. Clearly she had already spoken and had got no answer from the struck-dumb fool who stood before her for she repeated, patiently, 'Your mother. Was she Irish?'

Foolishly I shook my head but said, 'Yes. I think so.' And

then, trying to regain some appearance of sanity, I gabbled, 'My mother was alone, you see, and I am not sure where she was born for she died very young when I was just a child.' And then I was acutely embarrassed for no-one had asked me for this miserable history but, mercifully, she interrupted.

'I am sorry to hear that. I'm really sorry. So, what is your name?'

'Joe Bradshaw. Well . . . I was christened Joseph Conrad Bradshaw and my mother called me Conrad . . . After she died I went back to Joseph . . .' I could tell I was smiling too broadly at her. What was I about, confiding so uninhibitedly in this woman, although all I had had so far was one miserable glass of inferior Bordeaux, as though I longed to please her? As though I were a small boy trying to ingratiate himself with a woman onto whose lap he wished to climb. But I could not stop myself.

'How remarkable,' she said indulgently. 'Actually, I was christened Mary but then my father called me Molly.'

'My mother named me after Joseph Conrad whose books she loved.'

She smiled again, raising her head, showing her pretty teeth as she laughed and, as though to summon the gods to join in our laughter, she brushed my sleeve with her hand. And I was thinking, this woman knows something. She seems to know something that makes her so lively, that makes her laugh so readily and so prettily. I want to know it. I want to share it.

And as she said, 'We will have to write our own story,' I reached towards her and took her wrist very carefully between my thumb and second finger, as though checking her pulse, because I needed to touch the warm skin covering those delicate bones, just for a moment.

'In that case, will you have lunch with me one day?'

Molly was holding a wine glass in her other hand and she now raised this to her lips while gazing gravely at me over the rim as though to gauge whether this confused man was a suitable lunch companion. 'Yes,' she said. 'Yes, I will.'

And I could see, over her shoulder, Clara walking towards us and the rest of the world came back into focus.

'I was wondering where you'd got to, Joe.' Clara was dressed that evening in orange and a sort of chocolate brown; a waisted brown jacket and an orange scarf around her neck. I remember thinking, as I heard her voice and turned towards her, how good she looked. But somehow or other in the intervening years we had become twinned in misery. I believe a person who is drowning will often cling to their rescuer so powerfully that both drown. This was the nature of our mutual destruction for by now there was something dead at the heart of things for us although we never spoke of it; like the smell of the decomposing corpse beneath the floorboards that everyone is too polite to refer to. But our shared complicity kept us bound to each other; we remained a fond couple, trying to rescue each other, fearful of hurting each other. Fearful of offending, we lived like refugees hiding from a terrible truth.

'Hi Clara. Come and meet Molly,' I said.

And Molly held out her hand to Clara. 'So good to meet you.'

Non-adulterers, made queasy by the facility with which I switch from wife to mistress, will have little sympathy with me. See me there, sipping my Bordeaux, flirting with a new lover while my wife comes to seek me out. Intoxicated by the rainbow of colours that swirl around me I am looking into the dark eyes of my lover-to-be and planning her seduction as I introduce her to Clara. But long before I found Molly, I lost my wife. Don't think I haven't tried to understand it before now.

The human pebbles introduced themselves as well and we stood in a busy crowd while my heart thudded away in the midst of my own personal kaleidoscope of joy. You see, while Clara was all orange and chocolate with her blossoming russet hair, Molly, dark-haired, olive-skinned, was gleaming in layers of pale purple silk. She wore expensive-looking red shoes. She noticed me looking at them.

'A rather risky choice, with the purple, I thought. But then, why not take a risk?'

'Why not?' I agreed.

And she wore them again when we met a week later in one of those pubs down on the river where she began by saying, 'I shall call you Conrad, we cannot be Joseph and Mary, not in any language.'

I stroked her upturned palms with my fingers.

I held my glass to her lips and she drank from it.

'To us,' I said.

'To us,' she echoed.

Starting from that moment, I wished our conversations never to end. We were now securely embarked upon that venture of creating each other which is the basis of all true love affairs. As her lover, Conrad, I became someone I had never been before and she assumed the mantle of my creator, feeling her power, revelling in her power, to make or unmake me as it pleased her.

I have wondered about her dominance over me. So, she had my mother's name, and she used my mother's name for me, a striking but not by any standards grossly impossible occurrence; should it be termed a coincidence? Jung favoured the idea of synchronicity: events linked by meaning rather than causality. Did the name have a great effect on me? And she, too, turned out to be a fan of the great Joseph Conrad. Was that more synchronicity? Actually, the important question for me, in terms of recognition, is did she have my mother's face? Of course not.

Although memories of my mother's face are elusive, I knew she was nothing like this new love of mine. To me Molly's most striking feature was her eyes, which were not particularly large but which possessed a remarkable fluidity; it was not just that they were naturally dark and shiny but that they were also mobile and expressive. She had a habit of holding her head still while she used her eyes almost as she might have used another limb; to indicate, to mark, to draw attention to something and then perhaps to dismiss it, simply with a look from those dark irises and perhaps a slight elision of the eyelids.

Her shape, when I got to see her naked, was rather boyish. Long thin legs, narrow hips, small buttocks, small breasts, a broad muscular waist; she was not really my type. And so, I have to conclude that her magnetic attraction as far as I was concerned was that in character she resembled my mother. When I was a teenager I questioned Father O'Connor about my mother, having set the scene with a glass of his whisky after dinner.

'I only knew her as a member of my congregation,' he explained, swiftly. 'But I can tell you, Joe, she was a lovely young woman. Flirtatious, yes, pretty smiling eyes. You know the song, when Irish eyes are smiling? She was like that. And, I would say, emotional. Moody? Not really. Very little of the dark moods although she could look wistful. Might we say, a touch mercurial? Yes, Joe, I think we could.' And he took another sip of the whisky. Of course, I had also asked about my father but he simply smiled at me and said, 'Joe, that is a mystery that I fear we will have to live with.' All I can report is that the moment Molly and I met in that angular mausoleum I believed that that face was the one I had been searching for all my life. Or, to put it another way, Agnes had left a vacuum in my soul and Molly rushed to fill it.

There was one other significant overlap in our lives; she was in the same business as I am. She was a clinical psychologist. There are many different sorts of animals in that zoo, but the point is, she also used many psychoanalytic skills drawn from the art of psychoanalysis (for it always was an art, never a science, despite Professor Freud's efforts). And like me she was a sceptic. Have I witnessed it save one single soul from perdition? Have I seen evidence that it has cured one single malady? I think it is all a load of poppycock, as my dear Father Michael used to say. Nonetheless the work of that old Viennese wizard is invaluable, irreplaceable. It has provided us, you and me, with the most elaborate, intricate, elastic web of semantics within which to bounce and test the meanings of life to which we adhere; limbs flailing, mouths agape, eyes wide we leap and fall, like children on a trampoline, terrified but entranced, breathless, using, to pursue the unwieldy metaphor I have embarked upon, hermeneutic muscles we did not know we had until, tired of this exhilarating game, we jump off onto solid ground again. And, to change the metaphor once more, properly educated in this language can we not identify the charts that will lead us through the deep-sea currents and deceptive shallows that threaten our ships; and as we lurch and swerve towards each other can we not consult these instruments in order, obviously, not to prevent disaster but surely to understand it? And did someone not say that understanding is the only true happiness?

Chapter three, I think, of this little drama. Ten years have passed during which, in the manner of lovers, Molly and I have spent many fragments of concentrated time together. Sometimes we had days, sometimes only a few hours, but there was always a sense that we remained part of a longer, larger story of desire which yet remained to be told. This is the telling. I am now over sixty years old and this involves Benny again. Fellow psychiatrist and psychoanalyst. He of the rugby forward's bull neck and the curiously feminine small hands. The medical man obsessed with his congested nasal passages which he treats with a useless variety of patent medicines. He has a long-forgotten ex-wife somewhere in Europe and a wayward son, Charles, who came good and took up medicine and is now a respectable GP. Benny sports two posh cars in his two-car garage: the Porsche and the Merc and when he is not busy dosing himself with Robitussin he escorts a variety of women about town. Benny, ten years older than I am but who always kisses Molly on the mouth although she chooses to kiss him on the cheek. Molly once told me that she thinks he kisses her mouth because he knows I have kissed it already. But the truth is, for years we were, in a manner of speaking, a threesome and a devoted one so none of this really mattered. We were all content to rest within the warmth of the ambient friendship and, as we walked together through the dusk of many a city, searching for places to share food and wine and laughter, Molly would link arms with both of us and walk between us, not to keep us apart but to bind us together, safely, within the protection of her encompassing motherhood. There is always something maternal about a good woman's love, and I am sure she loved us both. Benny is a good-looking chap but he has never settled, not to any woman at all, and when we three returned to our hotel at the end of the evening it was to my bed that Molly always came.

But that is not the only triangle that I wish to think about. It is that more inflammatory threesome: Molly, Clara and myself, gyrating around each other during three uncomfortable days and nights in the lambent heat of a Bermudian August.

Psychoanalysts love large international symposia: these are the carnivals of the psychoanalytic world: the Bacchanalian orgies of our privileged little universes. This one could have been in Budapest or Melbourne or Lisbon; it happened to be in

Bermuda. Its location is irrelevant: it was nearly in Washington but moved offshore for administrative reasons. By prior agreement, Benny and Molly had arrived on the island together and Clara and I had travelled via a dreadful visit to her cousin in Boston. We had had a hard time of it there; at least I had a hard time of it and so I guess it is true to say that as a couple, our coupledom was under great strain. This cousin of hers, Roger, was – is – a famous and successful film star and a veritable lion of the stage. He lived in a three-storey house in Beacon Hill, fully staffed. The beautiful old house was full of PAs, secretaries, housemaids, gardeners, cooks; even, I think, a butler. I thought initially it was the staff that got to me. Clara, for reasons that escaped me, found the deference and the unending attentiveness entirely pleasant. I began to fret; and I do not think it was just envy of Roger's opulent lifestyle. The more days that passed I noticed something even more unexpected: she began to expand into her role as Roger's cousin; she became visibly more glamorous; her hair, now an artificial but tasteful auburn, began to shine and I swear her skin began to glow again with its old radiance.

Roger and his partner Jacob were exorbitantly generous hosts providing us not just with every comfort but also their time. They entertained us with stories of their outrageous adventures all over Europe; and Clara began to respond in kind. She told them stories of our rather mundane little holidays as though they were filled with some rhapsodic magic; although I could recognise the outlines of the events I could not recognise the emotions that she described with such lingering and detailed pleasure. She patted the cream satin brocade of the sofa beside her, indicating I should sit there, and then she took my hand while descanting on the virtues of our marriage.

She gleamed and giggled and her smile, always broad, although she had never had very good teeth, became even broader; she laughed and squirmed with pleasure and I could see that 'the boys' as she called them were delighted with her. It made me wonder what being my wife had done to her and yet, and yet, if she was dissimulating it was an extraordinary performance. I began to distrust my own judgement. I had assumed that my assessment of our shared discomposure was accurate. Was it possible that it was all in my own head and I was just projecting (as we say) my discomfort into her; endowing her with emotions which were more properly my own?

Naturally I felt very uncomfortable during that time and the only consolation I found during the days we spent in this exhaustively elegant setting, apart of course from the plentiful booze, was that Roger, typical of his caste and profession, was an indefatigable smoker. So I was able to light up as often as he did and even at these times Clara looked fondly at me as though, on account of her love for me, she could tolerate this peccadillo, instead of subjecting me to the glare I normally received when enacting this mortal (literally) sin. They don't make me feel well, I have to admit, but the initial joy of the first puff is unexcelled at a basic sensory level. The point is, by the time I arrived at the conference I had spent several days in a world which made me feel quite de-realised. I felt raw, stripped of my ordinary axiomatic assumptions about me and my life. If my life was not what I thought it was; what was it?

So, now we come to the compulsory gala dinner. I had woken up that morning uncomfortably aware of a depletion in my ordinary reserves and I was already wary. The gala dinner is always scheduled to be a night of excess and I was in one of my monkish moods when I am easily disgusted by too much consumption. At such times my ego defences are weak. I am, as it were, raw; lacking all the normal accoutrements of the average, solvent, educated, Western, white male professional. Social contact confuses me. I keep searching for the script that I must surely have mastered in order to be stepping out so bravely onto the social stage; all the other players are so well prepared and only I am at a loss, stumbling over my lines, embarrassingly stripped of meaning.

For the last three days, Molly and I had been circling cautiously around each other, searching for moments when we could be alone, hiding within the structures offered by the programme of the day. On the day of the gala dinner, I had felt throughout like a firefighter whose nostrils flare at the scent of woodsmoke. Clara was still in her neo-Bostonian phase and, to my horror, had started holding my hand all the time in the manner of those politicians and their wives who publicly clutch at each other like small children wading through deep water.

'Aren't we lucky, Joe, to have this time together?'

The enforced rest of these days was leaving her refreshed. She had never sunbathed on account of her pale skin but she swam each morning before breakfast and her eyes were bright as she smiled at me. It broke my heart to see her looking so happy and I looked away but she was not content to see my eyes averted and pulled on my hand until I turned to face her and she said, 'Kiss me, Joe.' And I did.

So it was that on that last evening, coated in ascetic righteousness, withdrawn and miserable, I said I would not go down for cocktails and, full of sweet understanding, Clara suggested we have a drink in our room. Like a courageous invalid, I sipped some sparkling water with a little lime juice in it while she, as befits a happy wife, had a large gin and tonic. As the dinner hour approached, with Clara clinging to my hand, I walked with trepidation towards the restaurant. The evening was gusty with ominous bursts of spray blowing off the reefs a few hundred yards from the darkening shore and the peaceful blue sky had become a turbulent mass of lumpy dark clouds racing towards the horizon. Night falls swiftly in Bermuda and it was now getting dark. We made our way down the steep stone steps cut out of the cliff towards the beach with a damp blustery wind lifting the skirt of Clara's dress and blowing hot salt air off the sea.

The Oleander Beach Bar and Restaurant was a vast semicircle of glass built out over the beach which must have had carefully positioned spotlights beneath it so that diners could look down onto the delicate filigree created by the breaking waves as they spread their lacy shawls over the pale pink sand. Then, as though choreographed by a master designer, behind each small row of frothy-skirted dancers emerging brightly out of the darkness came further and then further lines of sinuous shiny billows, no more than a few yards apart until much further out one could see the greater whiteness of the largest sea-going breakers, smashing onto the reefs, and then the even greater darkness of the immeasurable ocean stretching to the sky. While all this time within the great glass bowl of the restaurant, where the air was cold enough to cause a faint chill to run through me after the overbearing heat outside, there was circle after circle of round tables clothed in stiff white linen, sparkling with crystal and silver, delicately adorned with posies of small pink and yellow roses delivered, I dare say, in chilled containers on the flight from Boston that afternoon. We could see the wind rattling the palm trees outside while in here the candles burned with a steady flame.

Perhaps in the end the whole dreadful evening was about who owned whom.

Clara and I, hand in hand, of course, walked across the room and as we did so I saw Benny lean over to whisper to Molly while his hand tightened on her bare shoulder and he smiled his wolfish smile at me. Sitting in a spotlight on the side of a small dance floor, a gorgeous young man with a Freddie Mercury voice was singing some plangent melody while accompanying himself on the piano and in my pared-down, defenceless state the song seemed heartbreakingly beautiful. My heart swelled with self-pity: I felt like a man walking to the guillotine. I was still dealing with the astonishing realisation that my wife had been happy all these years while I was sinking into a morass of misery and believing, with an unseemly degree of comfort, that she felt the same; and therefore it was only a matter of time before we could safely agree to call the whole thing off.

'Hi Clara. Don't you look great. And Joe, oh Joe, I so enjoyed your paper. We must all celebrate. You're about three drinks behind us, you two.' I saw with foreboding that two acquaintances of Benny's, a former colleague and her husband, had joined the party.

We sat down. Clara on my left and the colleague, Phyllis, a snub-nosed woman of seventy plus and the emotional life of a child of six, on my right. Molly was opposite me. She was wearing a high-necked dress in a shiny gold material that I had not seen before and her arms and shoulders were bare and glowing from her expeditions out in the sunshine in the last few days. She had drawn her hair up and prettied herself with long earrings so that, to me, she looked impossibly glamorous. The waiter brought champagne ordered by Phyllis and paid for by Weston, her sad, silent husband.

A plate appeared before me. 'Carpaccio di tonno,' said the waiter. 'Local tuna, sir.' I looked sadly at the thin slices of raw fish, the rocket leaves, the sauce, the capers, and wondered why I was there.

My champagne was poured. 'I heard a good joke the other day,' said Benny, as he refilled Molly's glass. 'There were three psychiatrists who had reached retirement age. They met at the house of a mutual friend and were discussing their plans for retirement. All agreed that the benefits of unlimited time which retirement offered were offset by the disadvantages of the ageing process.'

He was not a natural joke-teller, but he was doing well with this one.

'You know I've always loved music,' said one. 'And I find

I now have the time to attend to it seriously. I go to as many concerts as possible and I am building up a good record library of my own. But the trouble is, you know, that as you get older, your hearing goes.'

Phyllis snorted; she could see already where this was going.

'Well,' said the second, 'I'm in a similar position. I have always had a great interest in art and I now have the time to attend all those exhibitions I used to miss and even to indulge in starting a bit of a collection for myself. But the trouble is, as you get older your eyesight goes.'

'I know what you mean,' said the third. 'I found myself a lovely new mistress recently. I took her to Venice for the weekend, and we were dozing on our bed in the afternoon after a late lunch. I got up to take a shower when, seeing her lying there in the light falling through the shutters, I thought, the shower can wait. I went over to her and kissed her and she said, rather sleepily, "Again?" The trouble is, you know, as you get older, your memory goes.'

As Benny finished his story the laughter billowed up from the table, seemingly filling the room, while Molly looked sadly at me and my eyes moved involuntarily towards Clara. Clara was watching the two of us, her fingers plucking at a bread roll, her mouth open with laughter, her eyes expressionless.

I held my glass out towards Molly. 'Here's to you, Molly.'

As I spoke the singer swung into a version of Stevie Wonder's 'I Just Called to Say I Love You'; theme tune of so many separated lovers and certainly one of ours and I heard myself saying, 'Would you like to dance?'

I heard a sharp intake of breath from Phyllis and she leant across me towards Clara and said, 'Would you not like to dance, Clara?' But to my joy, Molly ignored that and stood up. I could now see that her dress was a long sheath of gold stuff gleaming and glimmering as though covered in scales and she stepped towards me, a little awkwardly in her high heels. As I saw her silhouette against the backdrop of the sea and the small line of surf shining in the light she appeared like some astonishing little mermaid, falling into my arms as though each unnatural step pained her, so that I reached out to catch her and said, very loudly, 'Oh my darling,' as I did so. My recollection of that moment is that I had quite lost touch with reality. Even as I spoke I heard my own voice as though from afar and as she fell into my arms I looked down at the table of raised faces. Perhaps their mouths were moving but I heard nothing but the beat of the music. So we drifted off, my mermaid and I, and I cannot tell what happened after we had left.

A shocked silence, I imagine. I hope that poor Clara was consoled within the depths of Phyllis's vast bosom. I hope Benny poured her husband another drink or vice versa. I did not really care but focused on capturing my scaly beauty in my arms and shuffled off with her, at peace at last. And as we moved together, folded together, I thought, maybe all I have been experiencing is the normal madness and grief of frustrated love. My brain had been fizzing like a snowstorm and I developed an image of my world, my present world, this great glass bauble of a room, being shaken by a giant hand but then put down, and now the snow was settling, coming to rest, the air clearing, my mind calming. So I began to wonder if all this emotion, this disruption in my sense of self, my loss of faculties, my confusion, in general my unhappiness, was simply to do with the losing (well it would be, wouldn't it?), with the losing of this love object which I now held in my arms so securely.

And at that moment, echoing in my head somewhere, was Agnes's word 'shining'. I looked at my gold-wrapped partner and saw that she was indeed shining, with love, with desire, with joy. The whole package that I had wanted for myself so badly. Here it was, in my arms, at last. And I myself? Shining too.

We could scarcely go back so we went on: we drifted into the bar and drank our own bottle of champagne and then we went to her room and locked the door and stayed there all night. Towards dawn I made love to her again and I felt that sense of invulnerability we have when we have broken every law of our own small universe and so have placed ourselves outside reason and beyond all reasonable rebuke. Nothing, I said to myself, in my drunken tumescent arrogance, could touch us now, and I pulled the pillow over my head and curled myself against Molly's pliant back and slept the dreamless sleep of the virtuous.

But then, the world intruded, and things fell apart. We flew back on the same plane, and as I could not change the seats I sat next to the tight-lipped Clara. Molly beside Benny.

That should have been the end of the story: the shameful truth outed, me either noble hero or dastardly villain, depending on which side of the hotel bedroom door you stood. It was, however, only the beginning of the next part which was nasty, brutish and short. We got home where Clara wept for hours and claimed she felt suicidal and then really took an overdose of something and I found her downstairs the next morning, unconscious, so I agreed to go to marriage counselling. We got assigned a male counsellor, which was a bit of a surprise because I had expected some well-meaning middle-class female meddler. Sebastian was very tall and large and fattish and jowly with damp, pale skin. His eyes were hooded with heavy lids and at first I hoped that this might betoken some hinterland of wisdom but as far as I could tell he was simply half-asleep or perhaps a little inebriated all the time. He did not believe in saying much. Having introduced himself in a deep bass voice he led us to a small, airless room with three uncomfortably upright chairs for us to sit on. Observing us he would have seen me seeming to sulk while Clara fidgeted. The truth is I was trying to work out how to extricate myself from the marriage while doing as little damage as possible, and whether I could say this. Was honesty really the best policy? But while I was hesitating, Clara began to tell the story of our time in Bermuda, her shock at my catastrophic and psychopathic behaviour, my insanely selfish response to her distress, my lack of all reasonable concern for herself and her hope that I could be brought to see reason and that the marriage could be patched up. 'And we had had such a lovely time together in Boston with my cousin,' she said rather poignantly, looking pleadingly at me as though expecting some endorsement. 'Hadn't we, Joe?'

I stared at our jowly friend, hoping to see perhaps one drop of understanding leak from the half-moon irises which were all I could see of his eyes, but he simply looked back at me and sat silent, his elbows on his vast knees, his large soft hands dangling in front of him. I found myself wondering how his spreading buttocks coped with a relatively small hard seat such as he was sitting on but I know only too well my unlimited capacity for divergent thinking at times of crisis and I dragged my mind back to my dilemma. There was nothing else for it: I had to dive in. 'I am deeply sorry for the hurt I have caused my wife and Clara is blameless but I do want to end our marriage. The truth is I am in love with someone else.'

While the rest of Sebastian's body remained motionless, the big hands raised themselves as though by some superhuman effort and opened themselves out like some gigantic flower. And then the voice rumbled forth.

'Well, then. What are we to do now?'

'I don't want a divorce,' said Clara quickly. 'I refuse to give you a divorce, Joe.'

I looked at the floor; what big feet Sebastian had. Like an upbraided schoolboy, I decided I hated him and responded in kind.

'Well, then,' I said. 'What do we do now?'

After some more silence Sebastian stirred himself again, reluctantly it seemed, and, folding his hands once more, said, 'You have five further sessions booked with me. May I suggest that we do not make any final decisions until we have reached the end? But, meanwhile, Joe, I think it is important that you give us your word not to see this other woman until these five sessions are completed.'

Perceptual idiosyncrasy is an interesting phenomenon; what I heard at that point was, 'Be a good boy, Joe. Stay away from Molly for five weeks and then you'll be free and you can spend the rest of your life with her.' Wishful, magical thinking again; always my downfall. So I agreed and laid the foundation of yet further grief for all of us.

In our sitting room, on the ground floor, was a fireplace with a modish marble surround and a matching mantelpiece and above it was a mirror. Large, oval, hanging sideways from a chain, it bulged outwards; its bevelled surface criss-crossed with metal bands like veins in a baleful, ageing eye observing and reflecting all that went on in that room.

When Clara and I returned from our encounter with Sebastian she walked into the room, no longer poignant, no longer pleading, but fierce, harsh and determined. She turned towards me and said, 'Will you ring her now.'

'Who?'

'Molly.'

'I can't ring her, just like that,' I said reasonably. 'I will need to tell her, face to face.'

'You are playing for time, Joe. You ring her, now. Now.'

The room too was oval-shaped with a small bow window at each end and the usual suburban clutter of furniture. Clara sat in one of the armchairs on one side of the fireplace. I feel like saying that she lit a cigarette but of course, she didn't. She never smoked. But what every movement of her body, every tone in her voice, every expression in her face conveyed was what a cigarette-lighting ceremony would have indicated at that moment. Insouciance. The exercise of choice. Gratification of the self. Pleasure. And power. She had expressed no surprise so maybe she had known all along about Molly; but now that I had challenged the hegemony of our marriage she was in her element. She lay back in her chair, crossed her arms and waited.

I stood on the other side of the fireplace. In winter we had coal fires topped up with branches and twigs I could not resist bringing back with me from my walks in the wood behind the house; my hunting and gathering side then very much to the fore. Now the fireplace was dark and sullen, the pale green marble was cool to the touch. My mind, I recognised, was doing its usual tricks; flying all over the place, trying to escape from the expectations surrounding me. I looked into the mirror, its rounded glassy surface reflecting Clara from an unaccustomed angle. A stranger, a hostile stranger, she seemed at that moment; reflected in this eye-shaped mirror.

Not for the first time I recalled my dutiful twelve-year-old self, struggling with my French homework and asking my surrogate father for help with it. I had been given the text of Victor Hugo's 'La Conscience' to translate and I was stumbling through the story of Cain and his wanderings. I was dutiful enough to bring the work to Father Michael but I was arrogant enough to pour scorn on the poem.

'Ridiculous,' I said, mocking both the author and God. 'It makes me want to laugh, this idea of a giant eye on the horizon.'

Father Michael smiled at me. 'Now you may laugh, Joe; one

day you may understand how awful it is to imagine being seen by an omniscient being, an eye that you cannot escape, even in the grave.' And as is usual with memories, this one dragged with it a shadow of its own; what would that honourable man have thought of this errant son?

A leggy antelope carved from South African blackwood stood on the pale green veined marble of the mantelpiece. As I lifted my hand to stroke its shapely back, Clara spoke again. 'For God's sake, Joe, focus, can't you? You're just fudging the issue. What on earth are you thinking of, standing there, fiddling with that ornament.'

'I don't recall seeing it before,' I said.

'It's been there for years,' she shouted. 'Phone the bloody woman, will you?'

Vacating a relationship is like vacating a home. By the time you leave nothing looks the same any more. Books removed from bookcases, discoloured spaces on the walls where pictures once hung, dusty corners left cobwebbed by vanished sofas; it all is, really, unrecognisable.

'OK,' I said. And I did.

In front of the eye of God, while Clara watched me, I picked up the phone and dialled Molly's number. I got the answer-phone as I knew I would. I dreaded telling Molly what I had agreed to; like all masters of duplicity I was procrastinating.

I did not leave a message but the initiative was soon taken from me.

That night I moved into one of the guest bedrooms. I might have been cowardly in agreeing to follow Sebastian's timetable but I was going to make clear my determination to leave. I lay in the unfamiliar bed watching the unfamiliar light from the astonishingly bright streetlamp outside lie along the windowsill like immobile moonlight. If it had been moonlight it would have had a magic about it, so white, so bright; but coming from a newly installed streetlamp it was simply rather distracting and annoying. And I was pondering the irony of our powers of sensual discrimination in this way when I fell asleep and had a terrifying dream in which I was trying to outrun a beam of light which followed me down roads and across fields and threatened me with death or worse: I woke up too hot under the unfamiliar duvet, sweating, my head aching, and still the light was there. I thought of Victor Hugo's poem again.

I got up soon afterwards as daylight began to appear: while the kettle boiled I walked into the hall to see if the paper had been delivered. There was no paper but a small blue envelope, good-quality paper, with my name written on it in black ink in Molly's script. *Conrad.* I sat down before I opened it. The kettle reached the climax of its struggle to boil and the noise stopped. The letter was brief and clear.

My darling Conrad,

I have been thinking things over and I am going to go home for a while. I want to have more time to think and I expect you and Clara will need some time too; whatever the outcome is to be. I saw her face when you were getting on the plane and she looked utterly miserable. We need to try to build our happiness carefully; other people's unhappiness is a poor foundation. I know you will not like this; please forgive me. I plan to drop this off on my way north. Please do not try to contact me.

With my love always,

Molly

It was definitely her style. When she was upset, or angry, she would not argue or complain. She would simply disappear. I did not dare to follow her. In the immediate moment, as I stood there, holding the opened letter, I saw Clara walk into the kitchen. It seemed we were on a war footing. It had been some time since we had greeted each other warmly first thing in the morning; but seldom did I receive a look of such poised hostility. 'Are you going to ring her again?'

'There is no need. She has gone away.' And I burst into tears and walked away saying as I did, 'She feels sorry for you.' So even *in extremis* I could remember what would hurt; but I felt no triumph, only shame.

I went out into the garden and sat on the bench under the willow tree and sobbed. Even an acute mental representation of my idiocy and potential embarrassment could not stop me. Mawkish, sentimental fool though I knew myself to be, I realised I had trodden this path twice before. Once when my mother died and then again when Agnes had completed her treatment.

Five months later, during which, after I had suffered enough, Clara agreed to divorce me, Molly returned. It must have been an expensive restaurant that we were sitting in for the candles were in small silver candlesticks; the metal folded like ribbons around the base of each candle. And we had been there a while for the candles had burned quite low and I could see in the dimly lit room empty tables and hesitant distant waiters.

'You do understand, Conrad. Say you do.'

I said I did, but I would have said anything at that moment, and I lifted her hand and kissed it; first the back and then I turned it over and kissed the palm.

'Despite appearances, my darling, I suspect it would be easier for you to live without me than for me to live without you.'

The spell broken she looked around, 'We're the last, Conrad. Those poor waiters. What is the time? I've been droning on. I am so sorry.' And then she smiled at me and I told myself I must try to remember all this, for once.

So, Molly and I moved up here together, to her old family

home. That was almost twenty years ago and I am an old man now and I have been faithfully married to Molly ever since. I believe we are happy although my judgement has been poor enough in the past. But now, my former patient is coming to disturb my soul again. I believe that it was her presence in my life during that brief time of her therapy that led to me recognising, finally, that my mother had died. That she was dead. That even I with my exceptional capacity for magical word play could not bring her back to life. That there was no point in trying to recreate the bliss I felt when she held me in her arms that night. Nor was there any point in continuing to look for my mother in every woman's face I met. I had had to mourn her and let her go.

And Agnes (I nearly wrote 'my Agnes') and I are to meet again tomorrow. I have said nothing to Molly of course. I pride myself on my respect for patient confidentiality.

A strong egoism is a protection against disease, but in the last resort we must begin to love in order that we may not fall ill if, in consequence of frustration, we cannot love.

On Narcissism: an Introduction, Sigmund Freud

DR AGNES JOSEPHINE STACEY

The day of the Wedding Reception

I EMERGED INTO TODAY FROM a bad dream; not quite a nightmare but bad enough to persuade me that I was anxious about the day to come and more anxious than I was prepared to admit to myself.

I was watching a woman who was being held by the neck while a voice says, 'You cow. You stupid cow.' Suddenly, vividly, over the woman's face shimmers an expression hard to read, as though her features are dissolving, as though she is being viewed under water and then, as is the way with dreams, suddenly she is under water, looking up at me, her eyes filled with tears and with the water that also fills her open mouth and lungs as carefully, remorselessly, she is held there until she is dead. As dead as a dead cow which, somehow, she now becomes. I realise with fear that the woman looks familiar but I cannot tell what expression I had hoped to see. Shock, yes. Anger, that would be gratifying. Grief, no. But the words sound so good I say them again. 'Don't patronise me, you cow. You stupid cow.' She is now nothing more than a dead cow, washed away in the filthy flooding muddy river water, left abandoned on a rise in the land as the waters recede.

But I've never, ever, used that expression, 'you cow'. Never.

When I opened my eyes there on the ceiling, just detectable to practised eyes such as mine, were ripples of sunlight reflected off the ripples of water out there in the canal, echoing here in my room the layers of movement of the ever-moving early-morning river under the bright dawn sky. So I was under water, in a manner of speaking.

I closed my eyes again and thought about my dream. There had been a picture on the news last night, floods somewhere in India, a cow's bloated body left stranded on a riverbank by the vanishing water. So that was where the image came from. And who was this poor cow? Perhaps I was the poor cow? Stranded here on the riverbank, and I smiled to think how literal my dream was in that respect, but also stranded, even abandoned, metaphorically, on the margins of the social world I would be entering today. Unhusbanded, impoverished, a reputedly clever but only moderately successful academic, emotionally compromised, as it happens, by my love affair with the photographer of the occasion, whose wife, Ann, since I myself had invited both her and her husband, would surely be present. Ann the unknown woman. Ann, whom I had never met, about whom I knew so little. Only that she and Freddie had been childhood lovers, high school sweethearts, in Cape Town before marrying and leaving that city to seek their fates in London. Ann, who often returned to visit her parents on their ostrich farm near Oudtshoorn. I shifted uncomfortably in the bed; I found it impossible to think of Ann clearly. Would we have liked each other if we had met elsewhere? What would she think of me today, and I of her? I had been unable to resist one of my characteristically foolish impulses when Bettina had said to me, 'Do you know of any good photographers, Agnes?' and I had replied, 'Yes, an excellent person. Freddie. Shall I contact him?'

I stretched, looking for the reassurance that I find in the feeling of physical comfort that normally spreads through me at such times. I sleep naked now. In the latter years of my marriage I wore pyjamas buttoned to the neck and each morning woke sick with fear with tears in my eyes, holding them shut after consciousness had returned, postponing the moment when I had to confront, once again, that prison of a house. My kind doctor, Charles, had said I was depressed. For it was such a beautiful house. And the garden was extraordinary.

One of the sheets was so worn that the thinned cotton was threadbare. I could poke my finger up through the torn patch; so much of my life needed attending to, mending and putting right. The worn fabric was now so soft and fine that it lay like silk against my correspondingly worn, softened, crumpled skin as I curled within this second skin of sheets. There were folds of flesh lying now around my waist where long ago I felt the arms of a lover or two, and, not so long ago, Freddie's. But this morning the pleasure I took in these simple sensations, moving my hands down over the soft warm swell of my stomach, was contaminated by some prescience of pain. I moved my hand to my breast, palpating the soft skin, was it there, the insignificant lump? Noticed for the first time last night, was it still there this morning?

Uneasily, I scrutinised again the continuing, plaiting, ripples of light on the ceiling. That rapid movement meant, I knew, that the surface of the canal was being disturbed, by a boat, perhaps, a narrowboat, too early for punts, surely, or maybe even a large swan, or several swans. At this time on a cloudless June morning such as this appeared to be, the rising summer sunlight would stream under the arches of the bridge, a couple of hundred yards downstream, and bounce off the shining water onto the whitewashed walls of my small home and onto this ceiling, offering me a coded, mirrored vision of the river before I rose to inspect it. But I postponed this view of the river and thought instead about particle partners. This seductive term is used by physicists to describe the effects of instantaneously communicated influences. Particles, it seems, can move apart while maintaining a mysterious connectedness. The example they used was that of a person tossing a coin in New York and when seeing it land 'heads' knowing that a coin in London was landing 'tails'. Once I would have said that I could tell, by examining the ripples of feeling in my heart, what was disturbing the waters of Freddie's soul. My particle partner: once upon a time life without him had seemed unsustainable. And perhaps, after all, it was. I had decided a few months ago, soon after suggesting him as the photographer for today, that our love affair had no future and should end. I will meet him at Lippington House with Ann, I said to myself, and behave beautifully and shake hands and say goodbye. I will demonstrate to Freddie and to myself how mature and sensible I am and I recalled with incredulity that I had decided the time had come for chastity and continence and that I would remodel myself as a serene and sweet-natured older woman; complete in my celibate life, intellectually and spiritually fulfilled by my work, my thoughts, my books. But solitude is an art, I reminded myself, and it is an art I have not yet mastered despite a lifetime's apprenticeship. And I felt my eyelids beginning to close again in urgent search for the release of obliterating sleep.

And the room would have let me sleep, its kind, familiar shapes clustered around the too big bed; the overladen bookcase on the right beside the door, the small wardrobe packed into the corner, the three-sectioned mirror standing on the old dressing table in the bow window to the left of the bed, holding within its stained and discoloured surfaces remembered reflections of my body as Freddie undressed me, excited both by what he did and by what he saw himself do. But this morning there was an intruder, the dress hanging sulkily on the wardrobe door, a material representation of the respectability I would be temporarily assuming today as the mother of the bride. And then I reached out for my cigarettes. Just one. Today, I told myself, was, after all, a special day.

I opened the packet and sniffed. An old trick but it still worked. Yes, there I am. Down on the sands at Merebridge. A child on the porch lit with erratic morning sunlight, sniffing at the cigarettes left out last night after my mother and father had gone to bed. My feet bare, my body light and taut. Free in the way a happy child is free; with no responsibility except to stay alive, and that seems easy. Nothing else. I walk tentatively across the worn matting on the floor of the porch, curling my toes into the bare patches, lifting my small insteps slightly at the rub of the fibres on my soles, reaching the packet of cigarettes as the sun moves out from behind a cloud and its light shoots through the damp, dewy air and onto my perfect hand as it lifts the packet up from the corner where it has fallen. A sniff, an aroma, stored somewhere in my busy head forever, and my mother's voice, 'Bring me the cigarettes, Agnes darling. And come and have breakfast.' The only real memory I have of my mother. The only one. Not even the details of her face. Just the happiness, the cigarettes, the sunlight and her voice.

'Come and have breakfast.' A different voice. My daughter's voice. Dizzied by returning sleep, I pushed myself up off the pillows. The half-smoked cigarette, always disappointing but the ritual did not work unless it was completed, still hung from my fingers, ash accumulating. The light in the room has changed. The ripples on the ceiling have gone, sunlight as bright and sharp as the blade of a knife now slices through the panes of the bow window and gathers around the edges of the three-in-one mirror like a halo.

My daughter Elfriede stands in the doorway, her eyes full of reproach.

'I wish you wouldn't smoke, Mum. I really wish you would give up. And you know it is dangerous to smoke in bed; you were drifting off to sleep again. You could set the bed alight. Anything could happen.'

When I think about the reasons why I might have married my husband I wonder whether I was in search of my mother's unremembered face. The two holiday snaps I have, and the one formal studio portrait taken for her twenty-first birthday, show a rather beautiful girl with clear pale skin moulded to fine bones, a wide forehead, severe eyebrows, well-spaced level eyes, a straight nose chiselled at the tip and a soft mouth. My former husband, Richard Stacey, an elegant man, had just such a face when I met him and I cannot believe that I contributed much to the glowing beauty that emerges in the fortunate genetic mix that is my daughter. She is well-named. She is elfin in build, slight, with dramatically pale skin and thick dark hair skilfully cut into layers. If you stroke her head it feels like a puppy's fur. Her grandmother's features reinforced by her father's have gifted her with a lovely face. She knows little of her grandmother, of course. For someone of her age the war and the dreadful car crash happened so long ago it could scarcely be said to matter. And then, there is the youth. That angularity of chin and neck, the uprightness of the shoulders, the slenderness of the waist, the unveined feet.

'I'm sorry, Elfie darling,' I said, gabbling my apologies, trying to recoup some grace left over from last night, 'I'm so sorry you have had to wake me up. Have you slept at all? You look lovely already.'

'I'll go and put the kettle on, Mum.' There was disapproval in her voice but she was laughing as I pulled on my dressing-gown and followed her downstairs where I put my arms around her and felt with a kind of wonder her slenderness, the smallness, as it seemed, of her bones and the coolness of her cheek pressed to mine.

'It'll all be all right, Mum.'

I worry that my daughter and I speak a different language. For me facts are slippery things, as I try to hold them, grasp them, they slide around in their soapy suds and fall from my hands; whereas for her they are solid and reliable and you can lay one on top of another and build a safe house with them. But, sometimes, we understand each other. And so, while my daughter put the kettle on, I stood in the kitchen on the day we would celebrate her wedding with my customary if transient feeling of triumph and pleasure. I had made it through another day and another night and here I stand, intact and whole as far as I know, in this lovely room with almost all that I need and love and that view towards the river and, here, the purple-black geraniums. The kitchen was warm, too warm. As I pushed open the long French windows full of morning sun I could hear the flicker of wings as the pigeons that come to feast on the grapes each morning swept out of sight. The vine grew profusely over a wooden trellis which I had had erected over the small paved area here outside the kitchen when I bought the house for myself and my little daughter after my divorce. A small but significant triumph over the forces of dispossession.

No, the dress was not the right colour. And it had cost far too much. Fluid silk, brown and pale cream, like the reflection of clouds in river water I had thought when I saw the material. But, beautiful though the fabric was, these were not good colours for me. I had taken Nancy shopping with me but that had been a terrible mistake, for Nancy, a warm-hearted friend but an extravagant, inveterate shopper, had deluged me with advice in over-lit, over-heated fitting rooms until I, staring disconsolately at my own lumpen body, worn out and close to tears, had gratefully allowed this cool silk to slide through my fingers, watching it glimmer as I let it fall. Like moorland water, I had thought. And I had said, 'I'll have this one.'

Now I noticed that it had a very unflattering neckline. What would Freddie think? Would he think I looked older? I tried on the wide-brimmed dark brown hat decorated with a single, beautiful, creamy floppy rose. Not too bad but when I removed the hat, it seemed to me that my hair clung to my head in the most unflattering way. The car would be arriving in twenty minutes. I would put my shoes on downstairs. The heels were far too high and I dreaded balancing on them all day.

By the time I had dressed, Malcolm had arrived. Malcolm is a bit of a mystery to everybody. Like my mother, he was academically gifted. He went off to the university and never left.

I'm tempted to say, he never grew up. His college is Pembroke and he has done well, becoming a Fellow at a young age but then that was where he stuck. His subject is the Old Testament and for years, it seems to me, he was working on the Book of Jonah and the theme of exile. I asked him once when I was in my teens whether he found the idea of exile attractive and he said, rather irritably, 'Of course I do, Agnes. We are all exiles.' I think he meant from Paradise, as in *Paradise Lost*. But I have not had a proper conversation with him for years. I remember him being very kind to me when I was a child: taking me on nature walks with a little notebook and showing me how to dry flowers in blotting paper between the pages of a book. And he certainly supported my academic career. He lived in college until recent failing health required that he move to a small care home in north Oxford. He used to take me to college dinners where he would decline the noisette of lamb and ask for steak and kidney pie. He gives the impression of being perfectly satisfied with his life. He drinks a bit, but mainly wine from the college cellars which is, of course, of impressive quality. In the vacations he used to like to go hill-walking. Often alone but sometimes he would join a group. When he does it seems he is well-liked. He sings in several choirs. He may be gay although he has introduced me to several interesting women in the past. He is kind and generous and unfathomable. When I came downstairs he was chatting to Elfie who has always loved him. 'He's not odd, Mum. He is very spiritual, that's all.'

Elfie was wearing her wedding dress. It was made of a soft, wispy, copper-coloured organza, gathered at the shoulders and below the bust and falling just below her knees in layers of ochre and scarlet and orange. She looked, there is no other word for it, heavenly. Round her neck she wore my mother's pearls given to me after my mother died and worn by me at my wedding to Richard.

The car Richard had sent was his lovely old Bristol, a deep dark blue, spacious inside. Elfie settled herself on the fawn leather seat as though coming home. She looked bemused and charitable and I thought, not for the first time, that when people are happy they are generous. Malcolm chose to sit in the front so that I could sit next to my daughter, 'Lovely to see the two of you. Both so beautiful today.'

I noticed a slight slurring of his usually immaculate speech and wondered whether he had already been drinking. Or, could it be something else? I decided to check with him later but not here, in front of Elfie. She didn't need anything else to worry about today.

The smooth passage and general grandeur of the car seemed to have silenced all its passengers and I was glad to have time to return to my own thoughts. I was experiencing a kind of release. I had arranged myself on the seat beside Elfie with my hat and handbag next to me, the car door had closed with a heavy expensive thud, and the die was cast; an irrevocable step had been taken. No matter how reluctant I felt it was now too late to go back. But I was going back. I was returning to a world I had formally left a long time ago. When Elfie and I left, I had chosen to abandon all my former ties to that unhappy world, as I thought of it. Telephone calls soon petered out. Half-hearted invitations to coffee or tea or supper soon lost their spurious rationale. And I then embraced with a surprising passion my new old world: while Elfie was at school or asleep I took a part-time course at Reading to manoeuvre my first degree in Philosophy and Theology to a B.Phil and then took a D.Phil (on virtue ethics) back at Oxford and then, a real stroke of luck, I managed to get a six-hour lecturership at Oriel. Returning today to, as it were, the land of my marriage, where I had once been so miserable, I could not help but wonder what it would be like. And then, like the compass needle searching for magnetic north, my thoughts returned to Freddie. And to my dream. To that worrying speck of remembrance: was I watching a woman being drowned? I thought again of the ripples of light reflected off the river onto the ceiling that morning and I reminded myself that I must behave well today. What mattered was Elfie's happiness.

'What are you thinking, Mum?'

'I haven't been back to Dad's house for years. I can remember the garden so well but it must be changed. Maybe even the house? I was trying to remember when I was last there. I was wondering if my journey today is going backwards or going forwards . . .'

She laughed, of course.

'You are impossible, Mum. Is nothing simple in your head?'

I had asked to be dropped off at the church in the village. St Botolph's Church was an old Norman church that looked as though it had once been built out of grey sand and pebbles by a giant child who had left out all the difficult bits. It was oblong in shape with a rounded section added on one end, with no steeple but an afterthought of a porch stuck on one side. There, the child said, that's a church. And there was no-one to disagree. It stood in a churchyard marked by a curious disarray of gravestones: they were clustered in no apparent order at all at one end of the churchyard, again as though the child, bored with its building blocks and refusing to tidy them away, had stumped off to bed. The yew tree and its bracelet of a bench stood in the middle of this untidy mess of leaning and mossy stones with just a few newer, cleaner, shinier ones in the far corner where my lost baby's grave could be found. Around the stone grew the dark-petalled geraniums I had planted, echoing those at home, a constant and precious reminder. They gleamed sombrely against the green grass and the occasional daisy. I bent down to pull off the dead leaves and sniffed the sweet cheap geranium smell I loved so much. I walked on, drawn into the further depths of the churchyard, towards an old hedge which stood in shadow, untrimmed, its branches interwoven with wild white roses which filled the air with a sweet scent that overwhelmed me and as I breathed it in a movement caught my eye. A bird? An animal? I turned quickly towards it and saw through the branches, just for a moment, a woman's face, and on it an expression of such warmth that I could not help but take a step towards it.

Then I heard a sound behind me and turned to see a magpie dragging something out of the ground. I turned back to see if the woman was still there but there was nothing but that sweet smell of the roses and the overgrown hedge. How stupid love makes us, I thought, for I had imagined I had seen my mother. Just for a moment. Clear as day.

I walked around to the porch and entered the dark, quiet, calm interior. Here I sat, briefly at peace, allowing a thousand years of distress and joy, of anxious prayers and wept regrets, to seep out of the old stones and sink into my bones. Cradled by the years of human longing this cold stone space represented I felt warmed and revived. Through the window on my right streamed the bright summer sunlight, stained by the colours of the family crests set into the glass by long-dead dignitaries. The light lay on the stone slabs of the floor in rainbow-coloured patterns as though waiting for my daughter to step into the adventitious spotlight. Religious faith, I reflected, operates in the service of the personality. Malcolm had told me of his father's harsh sense of right and wrong and I could see that that sort of clarity did not fit here. Beyond and above the altar, against a kind of rosy brown background, smudgy brown stars were painted as though by a novice teacher for a child's nativity play. I offered up a brief prayer for my daughter's baby. Health, of course, and happiness, if possible. Or maybe the other way around. And I thought again of my beautiful son who had had no life in the end. How do I know he was beautiful? He would have been loved into it. Should I pray for him? Did he know how much I loved him? And, then, back into my mind, foreshortened by time and yet astonishingly distant, I could see us standing in the kitchen. I am pregnant. I am saying quite calmly, 'Please don't get so angry, Richard.'

'I have a right to be angry.'

'I don't see why.'

'Don't you start analysing me like that.'

'Please, don't shout.'

And he hits me. Of course he has to be angry. I have known that. That way he feels no guilt. And I have known he would hit me. Have I played my part in those events too? I wonder, as I watch myself staring downwards. A little blood runs down my chin from my lip. Tentatively I wipe it away. I know if I say anything else he will hit me again.

'You brought this on yourself, you cow. I don't feel the least bit guilty.' I look up at him. 'Don't look so bloody horrified. And now, oh God, we are going to have some high-minded dissection of the whole scene.'

'I am afraid of you,' I say. 'Does that make you feel better?'

He hits me again. My head sways backwards and hits the side of a cupboard. He takes me by the shoulders and shakes me.

'Don't you lay this at my door,' he shouts.

The reverberations of those few moments have never left me. It has always been impossible to calculate quite how fundamentally my sense of self was altered at that point. All I know was that after that small, minutes-long scene, I adapted to something I found hard to identify. I felt as though a piece of myself was missing or rather had been reshaped into something unrecognisable. Even going to see a therapist had not really changed that. In fact, I could never bring myself to describe what happened between me and Richard in any detail, even to Joe Bradshaw. Most of the time I did not even remember it. Unexpectedly, it was this ancient and holy place that had made a space for it, dragged it back. I could not change, now, what had happened then. No, I could change nothing of all that. Except the way I thought about it, remembered it. It was done. I had to own the sadness. And the shame. And the remorse. And the anger. And I had to be brave. And I had to protect Elfie from this knowledge. Didn't I? And, of course, this house was where the terror lay. By many standards, I had told myself even at the time, it was not that bad. It was that violent on only one occasion, but once was enough. And it may have led to the miscarriage. I had never been deliberately hurt before. I remembered only love from my parents. My grandparents had been gentle towards me. Malcolm was always on my side. Schoolfriends were easy. Boyfriends remarkably well-behaved. How safe I had felt when I had married this widely respected man and come to this beautiful house. How ignorant and foolish, I was. How spoilt. How shamefully cosseted. So I hid the memory away. At the time I had believed it was plainly my fault. I had felt very small and weak afterwards. And then, in the end, I did choose to go back to Richard. To this beautiful home. And I must remember that today is Elfie's day.

Lippington House is a manor house famous for its general loveliness, a jewel set in the village of Lippington in the bejewelled Gloucester countryside. Even when I had lived here, and it had been a prison to me, I would find myself overcome with wonder each time the car turned in through the wide gates then rose slightly over the bridge and the astonishing vista opened up before me. There, lying in front of the many-layered golden-stoned house, were the perfectly proportioned lawns with beyond them, the intense fire colours of the herbaceous border smouldering against the faded redbrick wall. And there was the pebbled river, clear as glass, escaping from the constraints of the steep banks beneath the small stone bridge on the right, growing wider and shallower as it flowed, winding towards the rickety little footbridge, past the banks where rough grass and shrubs rose to the warm cluster of beech trees on the summit of the hill. It was a sight committed a hundred times to memory but it had proved, as numinous sensations always do, elusive, vanishing.

This was really only a small wedding celebration. Theo and Elfie had already had a civil marriage a few days ago and a no doubt riotous party afterwards with their friends, and the gathering today was simply to give the young couple a chance to celebrate their marriage in the presence of their parents and other family members. When I had visited Theo's family in Newfoundland last Christmas we had agreed that Theo's mother should offer a blessing. It was, however, the intimacy of the occasion that I found challenging. It would be held in the garden of a home I had once longed to escape from and my decision to stop at the church first had reason in that I had wanted to mourn William before celebrating Elfie but I also knew that I had delayed returning to the house because there was a lingering apprehension. Of what? Of hurt? I could see at the end of the winding driveway the front of the house, the open space before it now filled with cars, the dovecote beyond, and felt again a tremor of anxiety. What sort of welcome would this old house afford me today? And Richard?

Involuntarily my eyes were drawn to the hill beyond the house where the summer beeches now gleamed green against the warm sky. I remembered a day one November, late in the month, over twenty years ago, shortly before Elfie and I had left Lippington House, when we had climbed that hill to catch leaves falling from the trees. It was cold, very cold, ice lining the puddles, and I held Elfie's small, gloved hand in mine as we struggled up the wet leaf-strewn grass. As we got closer I became aware of a hissing, whispering, susurration that enveloped the two of us: seemingly hanging in the air the sound was unchanging, never stopping, never louder or softer, its very persistence strange yet comforting. We looked up at the vast branches of the ancient trees where a myriad of last leaves, stiff with ice, still hung waiting their turn to fall in the windless air straight to the ground. Peering in the pale winter sunlight into the complex mass of branches, some several feet thick, winding like so many paths up, up into the distant white sky, we listened to the noise of the trees as the ice that lay on the leaves, now warmed just enough by the pale rays of the sun, melted, slipped and fell to the ground.

'Let's catch leaves, Mummy. Then we can make a wish.' But I was transfixed by the beauty of those old proud branches, by their imperturbability, by the music the ice made as it melted and fell, by the fact that for several hundred years people had passed beneath these trees and still they stood, patiently, wrapped now in this unearthly sound: the sound, surely, of the stars or limitless inaccessible space.

I did not want to leave that memory. I felt a physical longing to run back up the hill to the trees and to bury myself within the timeless cycles of their impersonal seasons. For still the memory of that time solaced and encapsulated me, even now that the trees were in full summer leaf and voices pressed around me dragging me back into the primary colours of the joyful wedding party where I now belonged.

'Mum.' Elfie's voice. I half expected her to say, 'Let's catch leaves, Mummy,' but as I turned to look at her she kissed me and said, 'Here is your new son-in-law, Mum,' and Theo embraced me and kissed my cheek and I followed them out to the terrace that edged the garden. The old uneven paving stones were perilous for high-heeled shoes and I stepped carefully, avoiding the cracks, remembering childhood games at the vicarage in which stepping on the cracks on the garden path was a sure sign of extreme danger, remembering long city walks when stepping on the cracks in the pavements was an absolute dread, wondering what, if any, connection there was between far-off childish obsessions and adult wariness when Freddie gripped my arm and said, 'We need to get the photographs done, Aggie,' and I looked up to see my four fellow parents and the newly married pair standing in a line on the edge of the terrace, facing the garden, looking back at me as at some truanting child. 'Where is Ann?' I asked as, avoiding the cracks, I walked over to join them and we stood there like starlings on a telephone wire while Freddie ran down the steps onto the lawn and raised his camera, telling us to stop looking so serious and to smile. I greeted Neville and Denise,Theo's happily married parents with what I hoped was an appealing smile, wondering what they would make of my own visibly chaotic relationships. 'So good to see you again, Agnes,' said Bettina. Richard moved forward to say hello and I found I was rubbing my arm, furious that Freddie had touched me so unfeelingly. I could see the other guests wandering over the lawn as, like a magnet, the river with its whispering charm drew them to its banks and they sipped their vintage champagne and marvelled at the wonder of the garden. I saw Charles down there talking earnestly to an elderly man who had to be Joe Bradshaw. I felt a kind of monumental sadness, not that all this loveliness no longer belonged to me, but that it had had so little good effect on me and Richard, when we lived here. I turned to look at him and I wanted to say something like, 'Are you happy, Richard?' but my courage failed me and all that came out was, 'The garden is looking lovely.'

'We've had a lot of work done this year,' he said. 'What do you think of the summerhouse?'

I looked at the further bank of the river where the ground had been levelled, the bank paved, and a small, immaculate, exquisitely designed two-storey building had been erected where once there had been a lop-sided old woodshed where Elfie used to play alongside the spiders and the faint smell of creosote.

'It's very smart,' I said. 'It fits in very well. It looks lovely. When did you have it built?'

'Not long ago. We've got a couple of old French fireplaces inside. It's turned out very well.'

I wanted to say, 'Do you remember the woodshed?' but fear of the cracks held me back.

Freddie had exhausted the potential of our current position and wanted to take pictures of the whole party so we were assembled on the lawn, on the slope beneath the terrace, the tallest at the back, the shortest at the front, Elfie and Theo in the centre with us on either side. Freddie was in his element, charming, coaxing, commanding, a positive stand-up turn, I thought, as he danced and talked his way around the tripod on which the camera stood. The assembly laughed and smiled and no doubt gave him the pictures he wanted. I had been trying not to focus on him but now that he was cavorting before me I could not stop asking myself, what was he thinking? And how easy was this whole process for him? Could it really be as easy as it seemed? And where was Ann? And although stories of love and hate are at bottom so tedious, yet I could not repress the insistent impression that I hated this man: right now I hated him for his insouciance, his bland exercise of his professional charm, his preparedness to play the game. But, I silently protested, I will not play your game, Freddie. Wait and see. I will find a way of showing you my displeasure. And yet, at the same time, congruent in every respect, I found myself wanting to ask, so what do you think of this garden then? He had never seen the garden before, although he had heard about it often enough. And I wanted to gather him up and escort him to the French four-poster which no doubt stood in the room upstairs in the summerhouse next to the French fireplace and say, 'Look, there, Freddie. Look back at that house, at its gorgeous reflection held in the river, look. Then kiss me and hold me. I am afraid and I am alone. Here I am always alone.'

'What did you say, Mum?'

Such was my earnestness, I had spoken aloud but it was Elfie who had heard. 'Nothing,' I laughed. 'Just mumbling. Do you remember the woodshed, darling? You kept your doll's pram down there and it was always full of spiders.'

A young waiter was carrying around glasses of champagne and bottles to top them up and we were each handed a glass and then Freddie walked down to the slender wooden footbridge which crossed the river and then up onto the paved area before the summerhouse. An abundance of pink roses spilled almost into the water from the edge of the paving and on either side of the small building luxuriant golden-leaved catalpa trees shed white blossoms. He beckoned to us to follow so that various combinations, mother and daughter, parents and daughter, mother and son, parents and son and so on, could be taken with the main house as a distant backdrop.

I am uneasy about photographs. I remembered my misgivings this morning when I first noticed how the soft folds of silk on the neckline of my dress offered a very unkind mirroring of the folds of ageing skin around my neck. And the patterns of sky and water so clearly visible to me when the silk moved and fell in the dressing room would in the sunlight, I knew, coagulate into ugly blobs when fixed by Freddie's unrelenting lens. So, it was a painful process for me. Again, for Elfie's sake, I submitted gracefully. I held my chin up, making my neck as long as possible, only to be told by Freddie, 'Relax, Aggie. We're meant to be having a good time today,' so that, if I had not hated him before, I would certainly have hated him then. Elfie and Theo were naturals in front of the camera. As was Richard. As we made our way back to the bridge, I looked up the hill, admiring the light which cascaded down through the beech trees over their wild spreading roots and the occasional violet pompoms of wild garlic.

In the shifting light under the red oak the long stone table beside the summerhouse was laid ready for our wedding feast. There were the silver goblets that I recalled from my former life and the perfect facets of expensive crystal catching the sunbeams, the crisp white and blue linen, all the evidence of my former moneyed existence. Small place-cards showed where we were to sit.

Theo and Elfie were at either end. Richard was on Elfie's right and I was between him and Charles. Bettina and Malcolm were opposite us with Freddie placed in a sort of no-man's land, as I saw it, between Bettina and Joe. He caught my eye as we sat down and winked at me. Bemused and irritated I decided to ignore him throughout the meal. Theo's mother, Denise, stood up to say grace. She was a woman with a natural dignity, as I had noted when I first met her; a soft Canadian accent, and her son's dark eyes. I recalled the tentative plans for the ceremonial aspects of the day when I had been visiting Theo's family and how I had encouraged her to play a significant part. After our meal, she said, there would be some brief speeches from Theo and Richard and, here she looked at me, 'Agnes, Elfie and I thought you might like to say something.' I looked immediately at Elfie who smiled innocently up at me and then my eyes moved to Richard. 'Is this actually your idea?' I murmured and when he smiled I turned back to face Denise and said, 'I would be very pleased to say something. Thank you, Denise.' Our glasses were filled with white wine and bowls of creamy gazpacho were placed in front of us and baskets of tiny warm crunchy loaves.

I took a deep breath. 'Thanks for giving me a role,' I said to Richard. 'Thank you.'

Sitting there next to him I could remember mornings when we were first married when we had brought our breakfast down here just to enjoy the view and the sunshine. I could see the weariness in his face now and a kind of worn-out kindliness. Suddenly, his preoccupation in those days with whether the milk for the coffee was warm or cold seemed endearing rather than infuriating, I had a moment of epiphany in which I could see this behaviour as symptomatic of anxiety: an anxiety perhaps that he was not going to be able to control me. It must have felt to him as though I was testing the boundaries. From being loving and suppliant I was becoming critical and opinionated. As these thoughts slipped into my mind he turned and looked at me.

'I couldn't make you happy,' he said. 'You were going to

be unhappy all our lives together. I could see it.' And I had thought he didn't give a damn about my happiness. I reached for my glass. 'And I am sorry, Aggie. I am sorry for the way I was to you.'

'Delicious wine,' I said, seeing that Elfie was watching us. 'And I knew I couldn't make you happy. I am sorry too. How young we were.'

'At least we had hopes,' he said, rather primly. 'At least we wanted something good.'

'And look,' and I waved my hand towards the group around the table, 'is this not good, Richard?'

'But I don't think you are happy, Agnes,' and for a moment I glimpsed on his face real remorse, real regret. But I heard this as a sign of my failure and I was not going to confess to any misery today, or ever again, I decided.

'Philosophically speaking, states of human happiness and good fortune can as a rule be compared with certain groups of trees: seen from a distance they look beautiful, but if you go up to them and into them their beauty disappears and you can no longer discover it.'

'Who said that?'

'Some old philosopher.'

How pompous I was but I was desperately scrabbling for the familiar wall of words I needed to hide behind. I knew I could not trust Richard. The old look of anxiety and irritation was back on his face. How I fear and resist change, I thought. How much easier it is for me to be combative towards him than allow him to be sympathetic and to receive his anger rather than his compassion. And my eyes wandered down to the other end of the table where Joe sat. He had asked me this very question once upon a time as I lay on the couch in his room and allowed myself to think and dream out loud. I wondered what it was like for him to sit here as a guest of the evidently kind and civilised man I had described as a monster and to see me again, so much older but barely wiser. He was sitting next to Freddie and suddenly I noticed how flamboyantly Freddie was flirting with Bettina, who was smiling and giggling and twirling her wine glass next to him.

Furious, I turned to Charles. He had always been an ally in the past and I knew he represented a kind of safety but also another kind of danger; he had been in love with me for years. How simple it would have been if I could have loved him back. We could have had years of a sedate and publicly respectable married life. By now our glasses had been refilled several times over and we had plates of cold lobster in front of us. Elfie had definitely chosen this menu. 'The lobsters are from the Bay of Fundy,' she said to the table in general, 'The very best lobsters in the world.'

'How are you, Charles?'

'I'm OK. How about you? What is it like being back here?'

I smiled. 'Why haven't you got Rose with you?'

'We split ages ago.'

I looked at his decent, even rather good-looking face and wondered why he was so unlucky. Is that how people looked on me?

'I see your former therapist is here,' he said.

'So it seems.'

'You did think he was good, didn't you?'

I said nothing, refusing to provide Charles with his longed-for sign of approval. I was watching Bettina and Charles changed the subject.

'Did you go to visit William's grave?'

'Of course.'

'It was a terrible time.'

I made a big effort to respond and turned to face him. 'It was. And you were amazing. It was a terrible time.'

'But you went back to Richard?'

I knew he was trying not to sound accusatory.

'The only home I knew, Charles. The only home I had left.'

There was an awkward silence between us while I remembered that he had offered me a home.

'But you always felt unsafe here. Years later you were

carrying Elfie around with you as though she were some small mascot that might protect you from the fury of the fates.' I winced when I heard this. What a life for a child. 'Or his fury? One day, there was a party at the house and you decided you wanted to go for a walk. The weather was atrocious but you insisted. You kept saying you liked the rain.'

'I still do.'

'I think you were desperate to escape and you bundled Elfie up in her pushchair and came out into the garden. You started walking down the driveway. God knows where you were planning to go, but I came after you. Do you remember?'

I shook my head, not wanting to admit that I did.

'You must remember, Agnes. I begged you to come with me. I shouldn't have done, probably. Anyway, you refused.'

I could not remember this, and yet I could see it all quite vividly. Now that Charles had painted the picture for me, I could see Elfie in her pushchair bundled up under layers of plastic. I could see myself, skinny, bedraggled, in one of my raincoats, the long blue one, I think, my favourite at the time. And I could see Charles, younger, of course, but with the same features only smoother, fuller. He had more hair then and it was getting soaked by the rain. I could see the rain driving towards us over the gravelled path which curled in front of us to the right and then rose to disappear behind the old hornbeam trees on its way to the gate. He was holding one of my hands; pleading with me. But this was not my memory but his. Absolutely his. How could I trust my memory if it could create fictions to fill in the gaps? And I could see it so clearly. I was definitely wearing my blue raincoat, made of a dark, very expensive, silky kind of waterproof material. It had a button-on hood which I had attached before I left the house. The hood hung around my face and as I stood there in the driving rain I could see the drops from the hood fall past my face and join the small rivulets that travelled down the folds of blue onto the paving stones beneath. I was not wearing gloves and my hands were cold as well as wet and the knuckles were red and I had my free hand on the handle of the pushchair jiggling it slightly so that Elfie, lulled by the motion, snug in her cosy little plastic-windowed world, was soothed and quiet; she, too, seemed to be watching the drops sliding down the outside of her transparent outer limiting membrane. I was looking at her while listening to Charles and, now that I was back in the memory, I could remember hearing him protesting, 'You can't live like this, Aggie. It will kill you. Come with me. Let me look after you.' There were shouts from the house, just audible through the noise of the rain. And the light was darkening: someone had noticed we weren't there. I wanted to ignore them but Charles, always responsible, insisted we reply. So, we returned to the unwelcome light and warmth and noise of the crowded house. I was sorry to leave our rain-sodden world. Except that I could not trust that it was my memory. I did not want to.

'You're not listening to me, are you Aggie?'

'I am listening, Charles. But I can't remember any of this. Or rather, I can remember everything. But they are not real memories. I no longer know what I can remember and what I can't. I am very good at making things up.'

'You never answer my questions. Would you not give us a chance now?'

As I hesitated, unable to find an answer, he added, 'Look. I know you have had quite a thing with the photographer. But I understand that it is over.' I was looking at him in horror; not that he knew our story, discretion was not one of our strong suits, but that he was saying my love affair with Freddie was over. So casually, so brutally.

'No, it's not over. Not yet.'

But Charles had seen my discomfiture and he pressed his advantage. 'Really not over?'

'Really not over.'

Charles took my hand in his two capable hands, as though sheltering a small fragile creature. 'Aggie, you must get away from all this. Let me take you away somewhere. A change of scene will do you good.'

It won't change the scenes in my mind, I thought. But he

looked so woebegone and, the truth is, I was afraid of the next few weeks. I felt as though I had discarded my safety net when I decided that Freddie and I should part and I was emboldened now by the alcohol flowing through my bloodstream but that would not last long. There was a terrible retrospective sorrow lying in wait for me on the riverbank in Oxford. As though reading my mind, Charles added, 'Is there nowhere you would like to go, Agnes? We'll get away for a while.'

Why is it always the wrong person with the right words, I thought, as I remembered once dreaming of going to Florence with Freddie and if he had said, 'Right. Tomorrow we go to Florence,' I would have gone with him. I would have gone anywhere with him. But I knew he wouldn't. And I looked again at the Freddie who was here today, on the other side of the table, who was sketching something with his hands to Bettina who put her handout to catch his while laughing her infectious laugh.

'Somewhere there are real memories.' And I might even have said this out aloud since Charles leaned a little closer as though to catch what I had said. 'Somewhere is the unalterable, ineradicable truth and I need not fear it.'

'What did you say, Aggie?'

He was regrouping his thoughts, afraid of saying something I disapproved of.

'My mother's second name was Florence,' I said. 'It's a pretty name, isn't it?'

'A very pretty name.'

There was silence while the sharp light of the sun rebounding off the crystal glasses hurt my eyes. I had left my sunglasses in my handbag. My lips were dry. The lipstick would have been long gone. The skin was tight on my cheeks and I felt a complete mess. I felt slightly sick. I had left my handbag in the house. I took another gulp of the white wine. If only he had understood what I was trying to say. 'You see, I've never been to Florence. It is a wished-for private joke between me and my mother: well, not a joke a sort of imaginary shared fantasy. That I shall go to Florence and I will find her there.'

'Shall we go to Florence, then?' I asked and Charles was saying, 'Wonderful! Aggie, what a wonderful idea. It's about time I visited it again,' and, encouraged, I guess, by my unexpected preparedness to include him once more in my world, he suddenly leant forward and kissed me, properly, on the mouth. And I, softened and sweetened after my recent irritation, confused and unhappy, hurt and angry with Freddie, warily and defiantly kissed him back. While I was pondering this, he put his arms around me to draw me closer but he had forgotten for the moment that we were part of the group.

So he turned to Elfie and said, 'Elfie. I'm trying to persuade your mother to come to Florence with me. I think a break would do her good.' And Elfie said, 'Why not, Mum? I am sure you would enjoy it.'

But the kiss had already confirmed for me that I could not possibly go. Behave well, I told myself, this is Elfie's special day and you owe it to her. And I realised that I wanted to see someone so strongly it almost stopped my breath until I realised it was, stupidly, stupidly, my mother I was looking for. As though she should be there. And, beside her, of course, the young Dutch refugee who had loved her, my father. They would have looked after me. Ghosts, merely, but oh that they were there on this day when I needed all the strength I could muster just to own my own soul now that I was back here in this place. These two faces I might have loved so much. Both still young, of course. Untouched by time. And I was actually considering rising to my feet to propose a toast to my loving fair-haired father as he stood beside my beautiful dark-haired mother, to celebrate the fact that they had had their brief hours of glory; years of wonder, excitement, joy and fulfilment, as I imagined them, which shows how much wine and champagne I must have drunk.

And then I saw that Theo was standing up and that Elfie was walking down to join him.

Theo is very tall and very handsome. His bearing and his

physique are inherited from the six-foot logger and trapper who married his Inuit grandmother. He was wearing a cream linen suit and I thought he looked like a young god, standing there, speaking to us all with what seemed to me like a vast confidence. Oh to be so young, so beautiful, so confident and so loved, I thought. How beautiful their children will be. Elfie was standing too, as petite as he was tall, but in her ochre-coloured dress and pale skin a perfect foil to him. They had obviously worked on this together and they had created a wonderful if sexist myth about Elfie as the spirit of the garden and Theo as the spirit of the world who would care for her and keep her safe when she left it.

Then Richard stood up. I saw with interest that the hand he placed on the table while he stood was shaking. However, he spoke well. Years of practice as chairman of the board, I guessed. The usual platitudes, of course. Beloved daughter, wonderful son-in-law, thanks to all the caterers and chief caterer Bettina without whom I would barely be able to get out of bed in the morning. A ripple of laughter. Any thanks to me for conceiving and bearing Elfriede? No, but a token nod to the part I played in a reference to 'her proud parents' today, with a glance down to me. Any reference to the son I conceived as well and the agonising loss of him? Convention, I knew, prevented any mention of such a painful event at a ceremony such as today's and yet, it made me angry that everything had to be glossed over and made picture perfect for what? Everyone here knew about that dreadful event even if they did not know what precipitated it. I had told Denise myself. 'He is still part of your family, isn't he?' she had said. 'I am sure he is always on your mind at family events.'

And then I heard Denise's measured voice, reminding me that I was going to say something too. What should I say?

So I pushed my chair back and stood up, the shining image of the golden house throbbing behind my unprotected eyes. 'I am a philosopher by trade so I am going to start with a philosophical reference. Spinoza wrote that if a stone that had been thrown had consciousness it would believe that it had chosen its own trajectory. I think my son-in-law would agree that stones do have spirits as well as consciousness and I speak now as that stone. I take no credit for the trajectory that brought me to this beautiful place, for having married Richard, given birth to my lovely daughter, to our daughter. I wish that her parents had loved each other better but here we all sit today and I believe there is love and friendship around this table. And forgiveness. I hope you will forgive me if I travel back half a century to the chaos of the war years, the crucible of my life. I find myself wishing with all my heart that my own parents could have been here today. First, so that I could indulge them with some of this luxury, secondly to try to convey how much I love them, but mainly just because they would have loved Theo and Elfie with all their hearts. I like to think that some of their legacy has found its way to their beautiful granddaughter Elfie, whose face bears a strong resemblance to the photographs I have of my very young mother. Someone who is very present to me today is our hoped-for eldest child, our son William. If he had been born he would have been four years older than Elfie. It is hard to be reminded of grief in the midst of a celebration such as this but he has been in my mind all day for this is the house where he would have lived and where I lost him during the fifth month of the pregnancy. Today I see Elfie triumphing over those early years when her life was overshadowed by the grief of her parents and making of herself a woman I truly admire, principled, brave and compassionate. In having you, Elfie, as my daughter; in being allowed to stand here today and express my pride in you, I have been more fortunate than I think I have deserved. But that is the nature of compassion. So, with gratitude, as a woman, as a philosopher and as your mother, Elfie, in this lovely place, I drink to you and your husband, Theo. I wish you long life and great happiness together.'

Everyone raised their glasses and Richard smiled acceptance at me, with perhaps a degree of remorse as well, and Elfie had tears in her eyes. Lunch was now paused while the first courses were cleared away. The desserts and the cake were to be served up on the terrace and people started wandering away from the table and I walked behind Richard to the back of Elfie's chair and put my arms around her neck. 'I love you,' I said.

She stood up and put her arm around my waist and said, 'Come on, Mum, let's have some time together.'

We walked over the footbridge and then left along the side of the river where there was a soft raised cushion of grass. Here we sat, side by side, our feet resting on a mossy bank just above the water and then, strangely, I began to cry. All the suppressed emotions of the day suddenly overwhelmed me for I remembered sitting, just like this, leaning against the grey-stoned curving sea wall beneath the promenade at Merebridge. I am sitting there on the damp sand and I am watching my mother walk towards the almost invisible sea, for on this part of the coast the sea will go out at low tide until it is no more than a watery streak on the horizon. So, it is low tide and late afternoon and the sun is dropping down the sky in front of us and there is my mother as she walks steadily towards the distant incoming tide. She is wearing her plain navy coat of good quality wool and her smart shoes, slightly heeled, laced to halfway up the instep. And most poignant of all, she is wearing her hat, which she wore to church on Sundays. Did I not wonder why she was wearing it today, when we have simply come to the seaside? And I knew this was a memory I could not have, for not only would my mother not have worn her Sunday hat on a day such as this, she would not have left me alone, curled up against the sea wall while she walked determinedly towards the sea and out of my life, and yet, this memory was composed of other memories I did not know I had either. Her coat, for example, and that green tweed skirt whose pleats hang out from beneath the hem of the coat, because the coat is really too short for my mother. I watch her walk across the wave-contoured sands, through the many small puddles of seawater always left behind in the indentations, and I see there on the sand her footprints: a long line of prints which disappear even as she walks. I watch her, hoping, praying, she will turn and come back. Surely, loving me as she does, she will remember I am waiting here for her and she will come back. But she is now so small a speck on the edge of the world that I know, although I cannot bear to know, that she will not return to me.

I can feel tears trickling down my neck, and I wipe them away with my hands and Elfie is patting my head, my shoulders, my cheeks, wiping away the tears with her own hands. 'Mum, darling, don't cry.' All this time she continued, with many small soothing gestures, smoothing my hair, wiping tears from my cheeks, patting my shoulders.

'Am I behaving badly, Elfie?'

I was fairly incoherent all this time, for tears kept pouring out of my eyes since although I was actually sitting on the grass in this lovely garden beside my daughter I was also still sitting there on the damp sand watching that diminishing figure and the awful reality of my mother's death, the unbearable knowledge that she really was dead, that she had chosen death and left me behind, that she really was not returning, all encapsulated within this dreadful yet precious memory, was flowing through me, I think, for the first time.

'And, now, I believe I can remember things. But I don't know whether they are true or not.'

Elfie was still embracing me, stroking my face, enveloping me with kindliness and comfort.

'What do you remember, Mum?'

'I have such a clear memory of it but I couldn't, I simply couldn't have seen this.'

'What do you remember?'

'Watching her walk into the sea. I can see her now. She is wearing her hat and she walks slowly, her left foot always turned in a little when she was tired and today she is tired. There is a cold wind and she has to secure her hat and I can see her footprints on the sand and I might even have thought of following her but I stayed there, as she had told me to.'

'So you remember it then, Mum?'

'I no longer know what I remember. I'm becoming afraid I am making things up. The thread of my memory is broken, Elfie darling: I am afraid I may be filling up the gaps with fictions.'

'But these fictions, Mum, may bring you closer to the truth than any of the facts you can unearth.' I looked at my pragmatic, practical daughter with amazement.

'Do you believe that, Elfie?'

'Do you remember, Mum, struggling up the hill one bitterly cold day: and at the top you stood quite still and I wanted to catch leaves and you said wait. Listen to the sound.'

'And did you hear it?'

'I heard something. Not, I think, what you heard, Mum. But I asked you what it was you could hear.'

'What did I say?'

'You said it was the music of the spheres. And I asked what the spheres were. And you said, the circling stars.'

'Did I?' I laughed, with pleasure, first that she remembered and secondly that I had said such a thing. 'But that's beautiful.'

'You say many beautiful, things, Mum.'

I looked at her and the whole weight of our unnecessary distances fell upon me and away from me and I said, 'Elfie, darling, I am sorry I have made things so difficult for you.'

And, as I looked at her, I wondered whether I could try to tell her someday what it was like getting older; what the inside experience of ageing is like. Not with resentment, not that. But the requirement, yes, almost the moral imperative, to grasp such gifts as life may unexpectedly offer and not to discard them as one is free to do when one is young, but to measure up to the challenge. Could I try to explain that when we are in love we are immortal? Could I tell her that however sordid the facts of an affair may look from the outside, from within it can be a cathedral of grace? No, my champagne-fuddled brain said, you cannot tell her that. I wanted to see some dawning understanding in her eyes, to hear her say, 'Mum, that's wonderful,' but I knew what she would see with those clear eyes of hers: a slightly tipsy mother sitting on the grass in her crumpled silk dress talking in a maudlin fashion about rather embarrassing things best kept to herself.

Chasms might be crossed but not in this way and, anyway, she was turning her head so that the sunlight fell across her cheekbones like a photographer's spotlight and I wanted to say to her, 'They were heroes, you know, both your grandparents.'

And I saw my daughter smile and wave at someone and she turned back to me as I said, 'But we can sit here now and remember the music of the circling stars: and it's all right, isn't it?' I did not want to forfeit one drop of this unanticipated consolation.

'Yes, we can.'

And she placed her hand on mine as Theo bent over her, smiling at me. 'May I steal your daughter away, Aggie? I've come to ask my wife for a dance.'

Elfie looked up at him with an expression of absolute trust and reached up to place her hand in his so he could pull her to her feet while I, rather than get up or even turn around, felt a curious and delicious apathy. I relished the feeling of my legs warm and relaxed on the grass and the sun shining onto my shoulders and hair and on my tear-dried face and I did not care one jot how I looked for a wonderful contentment was creeping through me. It was as though, for once, everything I was fitted perfectly, absolutely perfectly, with everything that I was meant to be. I felt complete. Completely happy? No, complete. My mind was empty except, if it had a thought, it was that there was more kindness, more tolerance, more sheer generosity, more grace, if one may use that word, in imperfect unions such as the one I had had with Freddie, than in many more orthodox partnerships. And yet, there was perhaps another thought too. And that was that I was only permitted to recognise this because all these qualities, kindness, tolerance, generosity, grace, could also be found in my imperfect relationship with Elfie. And this extraordinary sense of goodness was what was burning through me: something so rare, so unachievable in any purposeful way, I lifted my face to the sun and could have wept or laughed for joy. The white climbing roses hung in the trees above me like stars on a busy night and the river swirled past at my feet while the beech trees silhouetted on the hill maintained their solemn watchful silence and I lay back on the grass and stretched my arms above my head and, just for a moment, regained some of that childish sense of freedom and perfection that my cigarette memory had always brought back to me. I feel languorous, such a good word, I thought, languorous, and it will be, though lovely, such an effort to pick up this new life of mine as it lies waiting and to start living it. I will just lie here and wait. This epiphany, assisted no doubt by sun and alcohol, soothed and smoothed the ragged edges of my mind and I knew, albeit in a rather incoherent way, that this day would change my life and for a while I rested easy in that knowledge; it was sufficient to lie there, alert, fully conscious, yet free of the need to act.

The world, however, is uneasy with serenity. I could sense that this period of grace was threatened, would be short, would soon end. And there on the further horizon I could see, as I lay in the sunshine in the loveliest garden in the world, a broiling mass of fretful thoughts racing towards me. I opened my eyes, wondering how long I had been there and squinted up at the elderly man looking down at me, 'How are you, Agnes? I hope I am not disturbing you.'

'No, no, not at all.'

I was sitting up again and then he held out his hand. 'May I join you?' He lowered himself carefully down onto the grassy mound that formed my seat. 'I hope I will be able to get up again.'

'It is Dr Bradshaw, isn't it?'

He nodded, gravely, 'Much older but still me.'

'Bettina told me her sister was married to a Conrad Bradshaw.'

'Yes. Molly, my wife, calls me Conrad and now I am retired . . . You gave a great speech. I think I recognised the Spinoza?'

'It is very strange to see you here.' I was resistant to welcoming him and yet I was pleased to see him. I feared that he might bring old outdated truths and abandoned miseries from another time and another place and try to insert them into the small world I was busy creating today. For Elfie. For myself.

'You are angry. I am sorry. I was looking forward to seeing you again. Molly told me of an Agnes who was the ex-wife of our host today.'

'You must have had hundreds of patients?' But somewhere in there, in the midst of my unanticipated fury now that I was speaking to him, was a delight that he had wanted to see me again.

'Actually, I remember you very well. I was never sure how much good I did you but you were quite illuminating for me.'

'How?'

He stared over the river at the far bank but I was confident he was not seeing anything, other than his memories. 'When does patient confidentiality end? Some would say never. But these are my secrets not yours so . . . I was married then to a woman called Clara. And . . . after some dithering on my part . . . I divorced Clara and married Molly. I have been happy enough with her.'

'You mean I contributed to that?'

There was another long silence between us and I was beginning to regret my combative style when he added, 'Your story linked with mine. I too lost a mother when I was very young. About six or so.'

'I am sorry.'

'For some reason, Agnes, you reminded me of my mother. Very powerfully. After you left, I felt unreasonably affected.'

'But it was just transference?'

'Quite. But you triggered powerful memories for me.'

A damselfly was hovering just above my foot as it rested on the bank of the murmuring river. I stared at it. At its astonishingly blue wisp of a body. This was a shape-shifting moment if ever there was one. Joe my former therapist confiding in me.

'Look,' he said, 'look at that beautiful thing. That damselfly. What a lovely, lovely blue.'

'I was just thinking the same thing.'

'But I have a tendency to fudge things and I do want to have this conversation. My mother died, and I did not have a father. Or at least, I did not know who my father was. He had never been there.'

'Well, as you know, I did know my father. But he died too, so you and I were both orphans, young.'

'Yes. If your son had lived he would have been fortunate to have you as his mother for my mother loved me very much. Very much indeed. Just as you would have loved your son. As you love your daughter.'

'So, you knew I went back to Richard?'

'Don't you remember meeting me in the coffee shop?'

'Well, he is not a monster, as you can see.'

'Yes, he is a monster, Agnes. He is. He terrified you once and hurt you. However, he is often not a monster. And today he is a kind and generous host.'

The damselfly settled on the toe of my shoe. From behind us came the music of the piano and a saxophone. While Icarus falls the ploughman continues his task and the ship sails on. Joe looked at me so sadly.

'I too have been a monster, Agnes, in my time. Can I get you a drink? Wouldn't you like another glass of something? There is champagne on tap as far as I can make out?'

He was as eager as a schoolboy at a school dance.

'OK, then. That would be very welcome.'

When he brought the glasses back he said, 'Here's to survival,' and for a little while we sat there, companionably. The music drifted across the lawn, the roses hung in the trees, the sky was blue. It was all terribly *comme il faut* and I was about to say that when he said, 'Today feels a little out of time, doesn't it?'

I nodded while I said, 'I guess you saw me weeping here a little while ago.'

'I saw you here with your daughter.'

'I do not know why but I became overwhelmed by a memory I had never had before.'

'Could it be a version of other memories?'

'Basically, I had a memory of my mother; not exactly of her face but of her, walking away from me on the beach, wearing her Sunday best.'

'The last time you saw her?'

'Yes, it could have been the last. But I remembered that image for the first time today. And realised for the first time . . . viscerally . . . that she is dead. Gone forever.'

'Mum. Mum. Come and have some pudding. You will love it.' It was Elfie's voice floating across the garden as it had every day, once upon a time.

'I have been longing for her all day. I even thought I saw her in the churchyard.'

'Where your son is buried?'

I nodded.

'It was you, Agnes, who persuaded me that my mother was dead by creating in me emotions that made the fact undeniable.'

'Were you glad?'

'Of course. It is essential to get through that stage, to release the memories.'

I was now feeling at ease in a new way. It had something to do with this kindly wise old face that listened to me so carefully. And the fact that I did not need to explain anything. Or justify anything.

'You came over to me because you saw me crying, didn't you?'

'Not to stop you crying. By the way, I have not mentioned our work together to Molly nor will I.'

'Charles knows. And he will have told everybody. It's OK.'

'I mean, the contents.'

'Thank you.'

'I saw him kissing you.'

'Yes, he pursues me. But I am sure you can tell who I love?'

'The charming photographer.'

'Yes.'

'Maybe you are ready to love now?'

And I thought, what a portentous thing to say but at the same time, solitary by choice, I suddenly felt more hopeful.

'Maybe I am, Joe. It seems we belong to the same family now. Who would ever have thought it?'

And he laughed as he stood up, not without a bit of a struggle. I shook the damselfly off my foot, wondering if it represented something in the Inuit magic system, and took the hand he held out to me.

'Come on,' he said. 'We had better go and sample the pudding.'

Up on the terrace was a long table with a yellow linen tablecloth and on it an array of crystal pudding dishes and syllabub dishes and the wedding cake: royal icing of course. Also cheese and a Sauternes and port. I saw Malcolm smoking with Freddie who caught my eye and walked over holding out the packet.

'Here, Agnes, let's sin in public for a change.' They were Egyptian tobacco, my favourite. Hard to find. Still angry with him, I shook my head, not right now, but he pushed the packet into my hand.

'Where is Ann?' I asked.

'Not here. Sends her apologies. I have others,' he said, 'you take these. Not really my business but is your uncle OK?'

'Do you mean, has he drunk too much?'

'No. Is he ill? He seems to be speaking with some difficulty. Slurring his words.'

'I think he's fine.'

He was walking back to Malcolm when I heard myself call out, 'Freddie,' and when he turned around I added, 'The end was written into the beginning, you know. It always is with love affairs.'

I wanted him to say, 'No, Aggie, it isn't.' But he carried on walking and I turned around to see Molly and Charles sitting together a bit further along the terrace. Charles was urgently explaining something. I knew his body language so well by now. And I was struck again by how good-looking he was but that was something I could only see from a distance, when he was not trying to get close to me. And Molly was regarding him approvingly, nodding and smiling, presumably in agreement.

And then I felt a hand on my arm. Malcolm was standing there and holding out an envelope to me.

'Agnes, I've been wanting to give you this. Don't read it now but later when you are alone.'

'What is it, Malcolm?'

'Well, it is rather astonishing but it is a letter that your mother wrote, years ago of course, just before she died.' He turned away and I looked at the envelope. How strange. It was addressed to Joe. Joe knew my mother? I looked at Malcolm's retreating back and almost went after him but since he had seemed to want to make this private, I just put it in my pocket. However, a tremor of fear made tears start to my eyes. I was in a place where my habitual fearfulness had always needed to be controlled and unexpected events risked unbalancing this tenuous hold on stability. I did not go back into the house but walked along the drive, beneath the rows of walnut trees, until I reached the stone bridge and crossed it to reach the further riverbank. As I walked, trying to look casual, I examined these familiarly beautiful things: the sturdy coping on the bridge, the lucid brown patterns made by the water streaming over piled-up pebbles, the silver patches of light where it was mirrored off the river's surface. 'It is all right,' I said to myself. 'It is all right.'

Instead of turning left I walked across the paddock and up onto the high ground which led to the trees at the top. I stumbled up the hill, taking deep breaths, cursing my shoes, until I had the sense to take them off. The tussocky grass was cool and soft on my over-heated feet and when I reached the crown of the hill I walked along it towards that clump of beech trees which had long ago brought Elfie and me to the circling stars.

The late afternoon sunlight was now behind me and as I approached the trees the leaves on the low-hanging branches gleamed green and inviting, spreading a dense shade. I had to step carefully from one mossy spreading root to another. A long time ago I could remember the cascades of daffodils that used to spill down the hill in the spring but no summer flowers grew here amongst the roots now; only wild garlic and small fungi could be seen alongside the remains of the dead leaves of last winter. The elegant greyish trunks, smooth even in old age except for the oldest trees whose bark was beginning to fissure and wrinkle at the base, reached upwards as I had remembered but I could not see the sky for the layers and layers of leaves that after a while stirred slightly in the still warm breeze.

How wrong I was to quote that misanthropic old philosopher: these trees maintained every drop of magic even as I entered them and, as I had hoped, I began to feel calmer. One of the smaller trees must have been uprooted in high winds for it lay on its side, a tangle of roots exposed, many smaller ones broken off and sticking uselessly into the air but some of the longest, strongest roots still defiantly reaching their way underground, tenaciously clinging to the earth. These had clearly been keeping the tree alive since at its furthest end, waving no more than a few feet above the grass, was a cloud of leafy branches.

Here I sat on the horizontal trunk. How small I was beside these great trees. I stared down into the sunshine towards the golden house and the silver river. Like a dryad I could see without being seen and I scanned the lawns, edged on the right by the bright reds and yellows and blues of the summer flowers in the border and the climbing roses covering the crab apple trees, and also I could see into the walled garden and the rim of the fountain which I had always loved, and on the left the geometrically shaped yews and below me the river full of light streaming over the pebbles. This had been my familiar refuge and these, I promised myself, would be my real memories. I clutched my knees and looked down at my bare feet, old feet, swollen, now rather dusty, but the same feet that had once stepped across that porch in the house by the sea. My dangerous journey through this day was almost over. I took out of my bag the cigarettes that Freddie had given me. It was an old-fashioned box in the style that my mother's cigarettes used to come in. The cigarettes were wrapped in silver paper and there were five missing, creating just enough space for a lighter. I sat there and remembered my earlier fantasy and allowed myself to imagine that Freddie was there beside me and we were smoking and drinking together before going up to that imaginary French four-poster where I would say, 'Kiss me and hold me. I am alone and I am afraid.'

How absurd, to be afraid because a house looked so lovely. But I knew where these thoughts came from for it was the house and garden that had once seduced me with their loveliness. 'Surely I can be happy here?' I had thought. 'Here I will be safe.' As I remembered again that scene in the kitchen and Richard's scornful voice, I watched as the sun fell away on the left so that a shadow crept further and further over the front of the house, mingling with the creepers that surrounded the ground-floor windows. The slight evening breeze now drifted across the lawn and the river and lifted the smoke from my cigarette into the branches of the trees. I wanted to escape and I wanted to stay there forever. There was pain in leaving this place and yet a longing to do so as well. I wondered if I would return to this house. For christenings perhaps? Birthdays? But I might well never see it again; Richard had talked of selling it. Knowing that, I was anxious to leave and terrified of forgetting it. So I looked and looked and looked again at the picture of the house as it lay there before me, its reflection still burning gold in the river but in that reflection, as over the house itself, the evening shadow crept. I stubbed my cigarette out on the bark of the old tree and replaced the stub in the box and then I took the letter out of my pocket and looked at it. How extraordinary that my mother had known Joe Bradshaw and what on earth would she have been writing to him about and why had Malcolm given the letter to me today? The envelope had been torn open already so I lifted the pages of the letter out and as I did that I looked down into the garden and saw Joe talking to Malcolm. How secretive of Malcolm, I thought, not to tell Joe about the letter. And then, sitting there in my refuge beneath the beech trees, I read it.

By the time I got to the end, I could see, through my tears, my mother. Vast quantities of thoughts tumbled through my head and I did not know whether to laugh or cry. Here she was, in front of me, her words, her thoughts, her hopes and her love for me as well as the complications of loving two men. I could imagine the passion and excitement of her night with Joe enhanced as it was by so much danger but I had seen her myself with my father and knew how intensely she loved him. And here were descriptions of their courting days and my grandfather Willem whom I had never known much about or the grandmother I was named after. And life with my grandparents whom I had loved so much and yet who were always rather inaccessible. All day images of my mother had been pressing their way into my consciousness and now I could see her so clearly, except that it was through this mist of tears. Why was she so sure that Joe was my father? How could Joe be my father when he was my therapist? I wanted to protest that this was a category error. The quality of my distress reminded me of that time when Richard had morphed from being a kind husband into an unkind one, and my confusion then. People being discovered in a place where they did not belong. Like my mother being found dead. And my father, my loving father never returning. How could I make sense of it? And why had Malcolm held onto the letter for so long? And

I thought about the signs of ill-health that were crowding in on him and wondered if he had decided once upon a time not to do anything with the letter, that its moment had passed, but then, aware of approaching death, had decided it was a final responsibility? That made sense. However, I needed to make sure he had never mentioned it to anyone else. I saw no reason why Joe should ever know. That one night during the Blitz in that distant war need not influence our lives now. It was the past and should stay there. But how amazing. How amazing. I folded the letter carefully within its envelope and replaced it in my pocket. I would go and see Malcolm as soon as possible after the wedding reception was done with and find out then what the full history was.

After a while, I reluctantly walked down the hill and round the back of the summerhouse. Here I sat down on a sun-warmed stone bench. I considered squeezing my feet back into the absurd shoes but, having decided against it, I walked up the side of the house only to find a cheerful group around the table drinking whisky. Here the evening chill was far more marked. Cigar smoke mingled with the scent of the night-scented stock and I knew that this would have been my normal world except that now it was changed irrevocably. Joe and Malcolm were involved in a deep conversation about the war while Molly looked rather bored. I knew that expression on Joe's face so well: was it really possible that I was his daughter? I shivered. And Malcolm? No, I could not deal with these emotions here: not at the end of the day, not on Elfie's day, not here where I could not feel safe. I needed to think about this again when I was back in my own home. Theo was cuddling Elfie. I said hello to them all and crossed the little wooden footbridge again and as I limped back up the winding path beside the herbaceous border I saw Freddie sitting on a small bench, with my hat on his knee. The flowers burned like fires in the fading light. The scent of the star jasmine hanging in webs of white and green against the redbrick walls floated over us.

Freddie smiled at me and stood up. 'Hello Aggie, how did you get here?'

'I've been up among the beech trees.' But I knew that was not what he meant.

'I mean today. You and Elfie. How did you travel here?'

'Richard sent a car for us. Elfie, Malcolm and me.'

'And going back?'

'The driver is taking Malcolm and me home shortly.'

'Would you like me to take you home?'

'Can you?' I knew I was sounding quizzical and cross.

'I've told Ann about you, about us.'

I felt no joy, only a moment of fear. What had I done? For he looked anxious, my darling Freddie.

'I must sit down, Freddie. This path is hell on my feet.'

So we sat side by side while he lit a cigarette and then handed it to me. 'I want to share this with you.'

'Did you tell her everything?'

'More or less.'

'Are you afraid?' I asked. 'Because I am afraid. Afraid of what we might have done to her.' And there was my dream again.

'I'm more afraid of what we might have lost, Aggie. Do we still have time?'

'Of course you can take me home.'

And I leant forward to kiss him and then remembered the group behind me.

'Let's go to say goodbye to everyone.'

But neither of us wanted to move.

'Another beginning,' I said. 'Will we make it this time? Should we?'

'I am so tired of asking myself these questions, Aggie. I don't know, is the truth. I don't know but I am prepared to chance it. Will you?'

'Let me go and tell this lot,' and I handed him my shoes as a sign of ownership and stood up, planning to walk back across the footbridge. However, I could just see in the slow shadowing dusk the group around the table. Elfie had her head on Theo's shoulder, her eyes closed, and Malcolm, Joe and Molly were chatting together. It was a pretty scene, a comfortable scene, of family members at the end of a busy day of surfeiting pleasures.

Abruptly, I turned back to Freddie. 'Come my love,' I said. 'Let's go.'

I took his hand as we walked across the grass to the terrace where Richard and the rest were sitting. Together, we stepped over the cracks in the flagstones and I said, 'We've come to say goodbye, Richard. Freddie has offered me a lift home.' I kissed his cheek. 'A lovely, lovely day,' I murmured. 'Please say my goodbyes to Malcolm and the others. Special love and thanks to Bettina.' I kissed Neville and Denise. 'Thanks for everything.' Charles was nowhere to be seen which was a relief.

Finally we were free. We walked through to the front of the house and although I longed to look back I did not. We got into his old Saab with my shoes and handbag and hat in the back seat. He put the roof down and we travelled peacefully through the summer evening shadows along the narrow country roads. The slanting sun, dropping into the west, gilded the leaves of the trees with gold, staining the car with insistent patterns of light and dark as though a stroboscopic lamp were being swept over us as we moved through the patches of sunlight and shade. Beneath the trees bright red poppies stood in clumps in the long grass. The old feeling of safety began to creep over me again and I wondered if I had ever been so happy. When we got to the dual carriageway we went faster but still travelled at a measured speed as though Freddie wanted us to have all the time in the world to relish our togetherness again.

He parked in the old place and as we walked along the tow-path, I looked for a moment at the river, sweetly flowing, tinged with evening light from the sun now lying low towards the horizon. There were shifting depths of black and green visible beneath the surface net of gold and the sun-gilded reflections of the buildings around the river lay solidly on the water but there were no swans. Some punts had strayed beneath the bridge and now made their meandering way back upstream again, piloted by inexpert students and foolish tourists. All busyness was suspended in the curious timelessness of the river and there are no new words for this old phenomenon; the river late on summer evenings is always thus and there was no reason for me to linger. I shut the door and locked it behind us.

We walked upstairs with our arms around each other, kissing all the way, and my foolish dress finally found its place as a heap of beautiful silk when it fell to the floor around my feet and I stepped out of it like a water-nymph from her moorland pool straight into my lover's arms. We fell together onto the bed and lay together suspended in disbelief that we were back and kissed and pressed against each other as though a giant magnetic force had been switched on and we were being impelled together;

as though our limbs struggled to release themselves from the limitations of our separate skins in order to break through and enter the other's body and become one flesh.

So we ended up, out of breath, weary, gratified, finding, when we opened our eyes, that we were lying with our feet on the pillows; we dragged ourselves the right way up and collapsed again with his head on my shoulder, my arms around him, holding him as though armies should never wrest him from my protective grasp. And as we lay there in the warm darkness I felt the room fill up again with our love, my own damp body lying entwined with his between this worn-out skin of sheets. This is what matters, I said to myself. This is what counts. After a long while I said, quietly, 'Freddie, Freddie my love, I need to tell you something.'

He murmured something incomprehensible which I knew was assent and so I said, 'Freddie, an extraordinary thing has happened. Malcolm gave me a letter today that my mother wrote to Joe Bradshaw just before she died. She believed I was Joe's daughter.'

I knew he would not have heard me properly. He murmured, 'You mustn't worry, my love. You mustn't worry.' His voice was so drowsy. I released one arm from its protective task and, still holding tight to him with the other, stroked his hair. His breathing was becoming slower, more regular; I could tell that he was falling asleep.

'I feel safe now,' I said. And, curiously, laid upon all the other memories of the day came the recognition that I was never afraid when I was with Freddie; that this insecure attachment offered me all the security I needed. And I wondered, impregnable within my contentment, whether that was why I had never married again. Fear of the cracks. And this new feeling of safety prompted me to risk re-examining my responses to the letter. I thought about my mother and how present she had been to me all day and how, astonishingly, that awareness had been a precursor of the gift of her letter; so that reading it was almost like continuing a dialogue with her. I would have to spend a long time with the letter, I said to myself, I needed to read it with every care, remembering that it was she who wrote it, respecting her wishes, and then deciding what to do. Maybe, after all, Joe and I should have a DNA test. It would certainly settle the matter. And I needed to speak to Malcolm. How unforgivably he had acted, withholding this memento of my mother from me for so long.

Freddie's presence in my arms consoled me while I contemplated all the uncertainties that lay ahead. My particle partner, returned to me. But will you stay? Should you stay? I listened for a while to the rhythm of Freddie's breathing. He was sound asleep.

And I said to myself, he will go back to Ann tomorrow. And then I thought, he should go back to Ann tomorrow. But it was impossible to care about tomorrow for this moment filled everything I cared about. You will have to wait to see what the uncertain future brings, I told myself. Accept the uncertainty. Do not yet try to resolve it. The dynamics of the provisional. The end is written into the beginning. But for this moment, thank you, God. I hope that Elfie is as happy as I am tonight.

I must have dozed off for as dawn was approaching I opened my eyes again; I could see tiny threads of pale light around the edges of the curtains. I thought at first it was the pounding of my heart that had woken me but then I realised it was the steady beat of swans' wings as they flew downriver towards the imminently rising sun. Usually, hearing that tremendous sound, I would leap out of bed to catch that most beautiful of sights but this morning I sank further into the shared warmth of our bodies simply rejoicing in the knowledge of the swans' flight. After a while, I very tenderly moved Freddie's sleeping head from my shoulder to the pillow. And then, seeing the still-grey dawn light just beginning to edge in through the window, knowing that soon the first golden rays of sunlight would be sliding under the bridge, turning within the circumference of Freddie's arms, home at last, I fell asleep.

The part of the inexplicable should be allowed for in appraising the conduct of men in a world where no explanation is final. No charge of faithlessness ought to be lightly uttered.

The appearances of this perishable life are deceptive like everything that falls under the judgement of our imperfect senses.

A Personal Record, Joseph Conrad

PROFESSOR MALCOLM MILLER

Josie's christening

As it turned out, the celebrations at Lippington House last summer were very enjoyable. Before we left Agnes's house I had tucked Sophy's letter away securely in my breast pocket and was far from certain that I would not bring it home again to wait for what might seem like a more opportune moment. However, as I partly hoped, fate intervened. During the wedding luncheon I was sitting next to Elfie, of whom I have always been extremely fond, and we had quite an intimate exchange about all kinds of things including my previous love life, such as it was, and hers. Inevitably we touched on Agnes's various *amours*, considered from our separate perspectives, and I asked her how she thought her mother felt about being such an outsider at this conventional family gathering. Elfie agreed that it might be awkward for Agnes but reassured me that she too was keeping an eye on things. 'Although she is so good at hiding her feelings,' she said. Meanwhile, we were both watching Charles on the other side of the table who was trying as usual to flirt with Agnes who was, as usual, resolutely refusing to respond. Suddenly we were surprised to see Charles giving Agnes a passionate kiss and embracing her while announcing that they were going to visit Florence together. I was very pleased, for Charles is an honourable man and would have been faithful to Agnes, which is what she needs for a change although she does seem very attached to Freddie. I asked Elfie if she thought her mother would really go and she turned to me and said quietly, 'I don't think so. She would love to go to Florence but she absolutely hates being dependent on anybody. She would begin to hate him, you know, once they were there. I don't understand why she is so resistant to relying on anyone.' And then it was time for her to join Theo for their speech and while they were talking I reflected on the fact that, according to family gossip, Richard had treated Agnes badly as far as finances were concerned at the time of the divorce and I knew as well as anyone that academics are paid a pittance. I wondered if increased financial resources would help. It always provides more freedom. Maybe Agnes would like to go to Florence on her own. Or maybe she could afford to invite her own companion. I looked down the table and and saw Joe smiling at Freddie who was standing up to get a photo of the young couple. How competent Joe looked. And how confident. How authoritative. His demeanour confirmed all my initial impressions of him last New Year's Eve and I realised that this moment was significant. It was obvious that Agnes no longer had a place in this family, so she needed a new one and here was a potentially devoted father. I knew what to do.

I seized my moment after lunch and gave Agnes the letter. Although at the time she seemed rather preoccupied with Freddie, I hoped she would feel pleased when she had read it and I had imagined her showing the letter to Joe, who would surely be delighted. However, to my horror, soon after I had returned home I had a terse phone call that showed me I had completely misjudged everything and my complacency was further shattered when Agnes came to see me three days later. I remember hearing the church clock tolling midday and I had primed Sally in case another cup of coffee was needed. I had some sherry, of course, and was rather hoping that Agnes would agree to a glass of that and a few of my favourite cheese crackers to go with it. Then I heard the sound of her car on the gravel and I felt a little surge of, was it anxiety or excitement? Physiologically they are identical.

Those were her footsteps, characteristically quick, and then, in she came. Always elegant, she was looking rather tired. It was not long since the wedding reception and she must have been exhausted by that, let alone any emotional turbulence the letter might have caused. She gave me my routine kiss and immediately launched into a conversation but I tried to slow her down. I saw she was holding the letter in her hand.

'Agnes, my dear, so good to see you. Do sit down. Would you like some coffee? Or something stronger?'

She sighed impatiently. 'Coffee would be good.'

'Not a little sherry then? I have some just over there.'

'Oh, all right then, Uncle Malcolm. You are incorrigible. I'm driving so only a small glass.'

'Would you like to pour it? And one for me? There are some crackers there. I thought the wedding was a tremendous day. And I loved your speech. What did you think of it all?'

'The speech was embarrassing. Least said soonest mended. It was wonderful you could be there. Elfie and Theo were very pleased with the whole day and that is the main thing. Oh, and she told me she wanted to "keep in touch with the oldies" which is a little patronising, but very sincere. But Malcolm, I must talk to you about this timebomb.'

'Is it a timebomb?'

'Of course it is a timebomb. It has blown my life apart.

Reshaped everything. Don't pretend you don't know that. And, having squirrelled it away for so long, why give it to me now?'

'Because at the New Year's Eve party at Lippington six months ago I had a long conversation with Joe and I realised two things. First, that he has really cared about you from the moment he first met you, and secondly that despite appearances he is a good man. I guess, I also saw the two of you sitting on the riverbank talking at the wedding. Your body language, your whole demeanour, I don't know that I can describe it but you looked at ease, as though you belonged. Finally, you need a family member like Joe. He is a man of the world, which I am not.'

'We don't know that he is my father, Malcolm. What on earth possessed you to decide to keep this secret to yourself for my whole life?'

'I can find reasons, Agnes, good reasons, but truthfully, I am not entirely sure. That letter belonged to a different world.'

'And, you lived in that world. You were there while my mother was living through this?'

'Of course. And I was there when your mother got home after that night she and Joe spent together. Everything just as she says. And then her marriage to Kurt.'

'To my father. And she loved my father?'

'Yes, she did. But she also loved Joe. Wartime . . .'

'Oh, I know everything was different then.'

'Should I have kept it to myself? Destroyed it? I have not known what to do, Agnes.'

'How about giving it to me years ago?'

'But Joe . . .'

'It is not about Joe, Malcolm. It is about me and my mother. Such an intimate, open outpouring of her emotions? And you have had this somewhere, in a drawer? In a file? Tucked away until with astonishing arrogance you decide it is the right time to deliver this letter to me and then dare to tell me it is all about Joe. Who was never part of my family. Not my real family. And may never be.'

And I was quiet. Of course it was about Joe but now I could see that Agnes wanted to consider his involvement as peripheral. Insignificant. For Agnes her mother's night with Joe during the Blitz was no more than one, possibly unfortunate, event in the whole story of Sophy's short life that had led to the writing of the letter and the long explanation of who she was, and who Kurt was. And looked at from that point of view I could see why she was so angry and hurt with my secrecy.

I shook my head. 'Sophy was so sure that Joe was your father.'

'Well, I am sure he isn't. He can't be.'

How confident Agnes was in her fury.

'You haven't mentioned this to him, have you Malcolm?'

'Of course not. Once upon a time I considered giving him the letter but not since you have been grown up enough to handle it yourself.'

'I was grown up a long time ago, Malcolm.'

I quivered with misery.

'And why give me the letter at the reception? I never feel safe in that house, you know that.'

'I just wanted to do it as soon as possible after I knew you should have it and I knew Joe would be there.'

'So, you wait fifty years and then can't wait for another twenty-four hours?'

I felt demolished. I had never seen her so angry. Seldom seen anyone so angry.

I withdrew into what I hoped looked like a thoughtful rather than a resentful silence with a painful sense of how unfair all this was. I wondered if I could recreate for Agnes the circumstances of the time. Our wartime emotions, the constant expectation of death, the miracle of survival, Sophy's overwhelmingly joyful sense of life and then, so abruptly, the bleak hospital room and her dying voice, 'Then he'll have it.' And then, in a shape-shifting world, how difficult it was to be confident about anything. My decision after Sophy's death to maintain the status quo, the conservative position, believing whole-heartedly that it was for the best and yet, and yet . . . Could I now say to Agnes, 'But these were your mother's wishes . . . Her dying words. Obviously, she wanted you and Joe to love each other.' Was that not remarkably, even unforgivably hypocritical of me?

Should I perhaps have followed my sister's wishes and given the letter to Joe instead?

I watched Agnes sitting on the chair by the window, still clutching her car keys, staring out at my familiar graveyard view. I knew she was in agony. I knew she was thinking of Sophy and Kurt as she remembered them but more vividly than ever with all this new information about them. And she did not want to be here.

'The point is, Agnes my dear, at the end of her life she was desperate that Joe should have that letter. It seemed to be the only thing she cared about. She knew that you were safe, she knew that Kurt was dead and she wanted me to reassure her that Joe had the letter she had written. Oh you could argue that she was no longer in her right mind, shocked and shaken by the accident, by Kurt's death, by her own dreadful injuries, but the fact is, Agnes, they were her last words. "Then he'll have it." And the shame that never leaves me is: that belief was based on a lie. I lied to my dying sister. At the time I believed it was the right thing to do but now, I see things very differently. I now think it was criminal of me to decide to keep the letter to myself. But the fact remains that Joe mattered a great deal to your mother.'

'So, why wait fifty years for this all important news to be given to him? To me?'

'I needed to know that he would be a reliable father to you.'

She swung around to stare at me with unforgiving eyes. 'And what did my mother matter to him? Nothing. Not at all. Did he come back for her? No way.'

'Do you know that?'

'No. There is no sign that he did.'

'Well, you won't know for sure if you never ask him.'

She looked shocked. Was I being cruel? Something had changed. I felt enormously protective of my sister and the legacy of her death. Agnes seemed to me wilful and insensitive in the extreme.

'All those years, Malcolm. All those many, many years. And can sympathize with your reasons then to do with not upsetting your parents and what the neighbours would think and what you thought about Joe's suitability as a father but what about me? You said my mother left me in your care. What did you think I would need after she was dead? I needed to know about her and to know that she loved me as she did and it is SO apparent in the letter.' And she dropped her head into her hands and sobbed.

I was speechless. It was not often that people were so

vehemently cross with me these days but what silenced me was the absolute truth of her words and the pain I had caused her. How could I?

'And, Malcolm, these are my mother's thoughts, her intimate, confiding thoughts. As she says at the end of the letter, you know more about me now than anyone . . . and you have known all your life that I had only very few memories of my mother, her voice, the picture in my head of her with Kurt, and I could have known her so much more intimately. I could have seen the way her mind worked. What was important to her, what she cared about, what she couldn't be bothered with. I would have treasured these revelations of hers. About her childhood, my grandparents, her impressions of things, my childhood . . .' And she began to cry again. 'Can't you see how cruel it was to keep all this from me? As I was growing up. As I was trying to work things out for myself?'

'I . . . I . . .'

'Malcolm,' she went on, in a calmer voice. 'What hurts so much is that I loved you and I trusted you and I thought you loved me.'

'I did,' I finally got out, 'I did and do but Agnes, I . . .' and I could not go on. For the first time in my life, words failed me. I could not think how to put my tempestuous thoughts into any recognisable shape. 'It was because I loved you . . . I wanted to make up for my ignoring you that day after the car accident when you asked me where your mother was . . .'

'Because you loved me?' she gasped.

'I wanted to look after you.' And I stopped, hearing myself, despising myself, hating myself. How could I have got it so wrong? For there she was again. Small, exquisite, perfect, in my arms, her arms around my neck, 'I love you, Uncle Mally,' her cheek on mine. 'And I love you Agnes.'

'But I was never yours,' she said, 'I was not yours, Malcolm.'

'But we spent so much time . . . we had so many happy times, Agnes . . . despite everything we were happy together . . . we . . .' but as I was protesting, she stood up and said, barely looking at me, 'I think I had better leave,' and walked out, slamming the door behind her. What had I done? Immeasurable harm in all likelihood. I poured out a large whisky and drank it telling myself that I was calming my nerves. If only Sophy had been there. She would have known what to do. I pressed the bell for Sally.

After a couple of weeks I got a very brief note.

Hello Malcolm,

Joe and I have had a DNA test. It is positive.

Agnes.

I spent a long time after I got the note just looking out of the window at the church, wondering what St Ethelburga would make of my attempts at reparation, at restitution. I prayed (did I really? Well I do at times) that my unexpectedly tempestuous feelings after Agnes had left did not indicate that I had done something harmful, something else in addition to that early betrayal. What had I achieved? Remembering the emotion with which Joe had spoken about Agnes during our drunken chat on New Year's Eve, I had once more recognised the extent to which she inspired love for herself in others, without meaning to, I am sure, but just by being who she was. But Agnes and Joe had been linked together in one way or another throughout her life. Our languages for love are truly inadequate, I thought. And right now she hated him. But at least the truth was out and she was his daughter. Surely that was better?

What I have omitted from my self-righteous story (for self-disclosure always carries with it a whiff of the martyr) is that over the fifteen years following Sophy's death I became, I relished becoming, for Agnes a very significant love object. I thought of it as my act of reparation for the failure to respond when she turned to me for consolation on the day after her parents had died.

I had developed a new routine around my visits back home. I invented an interest in wildflowers and would take her for nature walks and I would buy books for her and read them to her. Once, I took her to a funfair in Southport and we went on the helter-skelter together and she clung to me shrieking in fear and delight and I can remember the sensation of absolute joy when I felt her fingers clutching at my jacket. 'Hold me tight, Uncle Mally!' I bought her an ice cream tub and we sat on the sea wall and listened to the gulls. I took her on the dodgems: she sat securely between my legs and put her hands on the wheel as I wrestled it around, laughing with pleasure as we careered into and away from the other cars. I felt so powerful. And I felt so powerfully good. And sometimes I thought again of Joe but decided that Sophy would have wanted me to look after Agnes while she was so young. Of course, it would have been quite possible for Joe to have visited too; however, I argued to myself, how embarrassing for my parents, still in mourning for a legitimate son-in-law, to have to explain to neighbours who Agnes's illegitimate father was, if indeed he was her father at all. And I reframed the letter as that romantically foolish notion that Sophy had indulged in and decided nothing but harm would come of delivering it.

As she grew older I would collect Agnes at weekends and take her to art galleries, concerts, films. We went to Liverpool and sometimes London. When she was older I took her to dine at my college. And, of course, she was often taken for my daughter. 'No,' I would smile at the polite enquiry, 'my niece. But a very special niece,' and I hoped the interrogator would leave with a sense of what a kind and generous uncle I was. The truth is, as I can now see, this was a proprietary move. I could have contacted Joe once the atmosphere at home was calmer. I could at the very least have looked him up myself. But I did not. Like a jealous lover I protected my innocent child from the fact that she might have had a living father, and allowed myself to feel good about it.

'You are the father she doesn't have,' said my mother. 'What would she do without you?'

A couple of months later Charles rang up to ask if he could visit. I was very pleased since Charles is as good company as an indiscreet gossiper can be. I think it could be said of him that he was one of those people who believe that treating a piece of information as confidential meant only telling one person at a time. However, I did not believe there was a single grain of malice in him but simply, I would have said, a consuming interest in other people's affairs. To some extent this was startingly borne out during the afternoon he spent with me. I knew, of course, that he was coming to see me partly out of genuine kindness. He believed that old people need visits and there was also a residue of the local physician left in him; in his day doctors did home visits. Nonetheless, it was with a real sense of anticipation that I asked Sally to provide a 'simple' tea for two. Naturally, we got both cucumber sandwiches and a Victoria sponge cake.

Charles was looking very sleek and cheerful. He greeted me with his customary warmth but I felt that there was an extra level to his cheerfulness this time. He was more of an elder statesman and less of an apprentice to the role. After shaking my hand he sat his solid, respectable self in the armchair placed for him and, for a moment, placed his fatherly doctor's hand on my knee. 'Sorry to hear about your recent troubles, old man. I understand your heart is playing up.'

'That's true, Charles, but don't try to seduce me into talking about all my old man heart problems. That could go on all afternoon and it is your heart I am more interested in. I have heard on the grapevine that you have finally settled down.'

'Indeed, Malcolm. I had begun to fear it would never happen.'

And he poured out our tea and took a cucumber sandwich and began to talk.

'The way I think about it, Malcolm, and, of course, Molly and I have talked endlessly about it, I always felt sort of in the second league as far as my life was concerned. I could never put my finger on it but it was particularly present whenever I was around Richard's family, as though they did me an enormous favour by including me in their social life. And maybe they did. After all. I was only the family doctor but I was a friend first. We met as students and had shared quite a few drunken student nights. However, Richard always was rather grand, you know, and Agnes was just so lovely and, and I can tell you this for a fact, so bloody unhappy. I felt called upon to look after her which is ridiculous since she is far more capable than I am.'

And I have to say I agreed with him, but wordlessly.

'When Molly and I started talking at the wedding we realised we both felt similarly edged out of being the important people not only at that particular party but in life. I don't know, Malcolm, I think it is just that we found an echo in each other of feelings that were difficult to describe. So, we stayed in touch, as they say. I don't think her marriage to Joe had turned out that well although both were too proud to admit it at first: it had looked like such a dream pairing and Molly had had to wait so long for him, you know?'

I nodded.

'The way we described it to ourselves was this: everyone is, surely, the main character in their own lives. You know what I mean. Each of us can see ourselves in the drama of our lives and each of us is the main character: if you like, the hero or the heroine of that story. And yet, when I analysed this with Molly, and she is really rather good at this, you know, it has been her job for years, when I thought about it in more depth I have always felt as though another person was the hero or heroine of my life story. It used to be my mother, I think, but for years it was Agnes. I became, had become, a peripheral character in my own life!'

His handsome face was flushed with passion.

'And Molly said she could only analyse this for me because she had also fallen into that secondary place in her own life. She had wrapped all her interests and concerns around Joe so that being with him was the only thing that provided her with life. Isn't that extraordinary, Malcolm? So, we felt it was miraculous that we had found each other, just in time, really, to have a proper life and put ourselves on stage as the principal character. Together, of course.'

If I felt that there was a logical paradox in that reasoning it was not for me to point it out. I looked at his good doctor's hands, now gripping his knees, and hoped that Molly was enjoying the full benefits of them.

'Do you know what I mean, Malcolm? Am I making sense?'

I nodded again. 'Of course, Charles. Perfect sense.'

'Then, the culmination was the letter. I think Agnes had stage-managed it a bit. She invited him down to Oxford; they had reconnected at the wedding and she gave him to understand there was something important she wanted to talk to him about. You know, Joe would have gone anywhere for her. And what upset Molly so much was that Joe lied to her about going south.

He said he was going to see Benny who is just about alive in a care home and instead went to Oxford to meet Agnes. They met in a restaurant in the high street and apparently she just handed him the letter. Who knows what passed between them. But Molly said when Joe returned home he was changed. In theory they could have gone on just as they were but Joe said he wanted to do the DNA test and when the results came through positive he decided he needed to live near Agnes! I have wasted so much time, he said. I need to see her as much as possible. That is so strange, Malcolm, you have to admit that.'

'Wasted time'. The concept burned a hole in my heart like watching cigarette ash fall onto a cotton sheet. A magpie fluttered around the trees in the churchyard as I recalled Lear's dream of life at the end with Cordelia 'so we'll live, and pray and sing and tell old tales, and laugh at gilded butterflies . . .' and then the cruellest lines: 'Thou'lt come no more, never, never, never, never, never . . .' Fathers and daughters. A certain kind of visceral passion which is probably not replicated elsewhere. Could this be what Joe had sensed and was fumbling his way towards when he spoke with such passion of his love for Agnes during our conversation on New Year's Eve? What might it be like, I asked myself, to have had such a daughter, possibly like Agnes?

Nonetheless, I shared none of this with Charles but simply

nodded and agreed it was mighty strange. Charles, however, had not finished and with a newly acquired and devastating candour he pursued his subject. 'And I have begun to wonder about you, old man, whether you might have found yourself in just such an unrewarding place?'

I was horrified. Charles was stepping out of role. 'What do you mean, Charles?'

'Well, when Agnes married Richard I saw quite a lot of her as the family GP and Richard's old friend from student days and she said how good you were to her as she grew up. "Like the father I didn't have," but when we do that sort of thing, as I did pursuing her for years, always trying to persuade her to love me, are we not hitching a ride in someone else's life that we are not entitled to?'

I was aghast. Molly was obviously doing Charles a lot of good; he had moved from being the extra person at the feast to claiming a central role for himself.

'I hadn't quite thought about it like that,' I mumbled.

'We all do it,' he said as though to console me, 'until we find our own place in the world. The one we are entitled to.'

'And have you seen Joe since?' I asked, desperate to change the subject. 'It is a difficult time for us now that he knows how long I have been holding this secret for.'

But Charles's words stung. They were true, I could see that.

This will not seem a great sin to some. In the context of the time it caused no further deaths. There was not much drama. It could have been described as a small venial sin. A sin of selfishness. Of narrow-mindedness. How curiously what I had thought of as my virtue had become with time a scurrilously damaging intervention in someone else's life, in two other lives, which I had through sheer chance had under my control. How pleased I had been with myself as I had inserted my way into Agnes's life and had acted the role of father and how virtuous it had looked.

If I had been able to cry I would have done but my eyes and throat were dry. There was nothing in me that supported life. After Charles had gone I sat still and stared out of the window for a long, long time.

When had it begun, this transformation of a boy into a toadlet? Was it when I began to realise that my father loved Sophy more than he loved me? Far more than he loved me? And was there ever a time when I did not know that? Was it that she had always had charm and I was born charmless? And then, I remembered my envy of Sophy when I saw her the day before she died. Her sense of life. Her excitement, her evident arousal, 'Mally, we made love ALL night.'

And the devotion that Kurt felt for her, and then the love that she felt for Joe.

How gifted she had been by fate. Or was it God? It was never her intellect I envied, dry, mechanical thing that now seemed, but her gift for joy. For deep joy. And I had touched the skirts of it that afternoon on the slow train back to Merebridge when Agnes had loved me.

Then I wrote a letter. A brief one.

Dear Agnes,

I am very very sorry for the wasted years that kept you from the knowledge of your mother. And kept you and Joe apart.

I was wrong and I can see that now.

I can only ask you two to forgive me, if possible.

With my love always,

Malcolm

Then I threw it away. The days and then the weeks and then the months passed as the world turned and I made myself wait and keep silent.

In mid-December I got a card and a Christmas letter from Agnes, dutiful as ever, a little colder than usual. She and Joe had been invited to join Elfie and Theo for Christmas lunch. Charles wrote his usual card but this time saying that he and Molly were in Switzerland and having a wonderful time. Picture of both with their arms around each other and a snowy peak behind them. I and my fellow inmates were given a very good Christmas dinner on Christmas Eve as the staff had the next day off and then some of us, fortified by an excellent port, decided to struggle over to midnight mass at St Ethelburga's. There had been a sprinkling of snow which not only made the whole churchyard exceptionally pretty but the journey there a little risky for us. It was the last time I made the journey over there on my own legs albeit supported by one of my mates. We linked arms and hoped for the best. The little church was lit with candles and I listened to the old familiar words with misgiving. Absolution. Redemption. Did I believe it? Did it matter? That night they used the BCP liturgy and as I listened to the beautiful old rhythms I thought I could hear my father's voice. Did this creed comfort him in the end? I hoped so. The sonorous phrases that shaped my childhood rolled over me with a mixture of comfort and rebuke.

After a few more weeks of torture, I knew I had been partially forgiven when they came to see me, the new family. Joe, Agnes, Elfie. Soon to be a four-generation family. We all had tea in my room. Sally laid on cucumber sandwiches and scones this time as well as a Victoria sponge on a triple-tiered cake stand. It all felt curiously formal. It was, after all, a new world. You could say, and I think I did, that the horizon had changed. Joe greeted me with an awkward sort of embrace as an attempt to represent our changed relationship.

'Little did we know, Malcolm, when we met that New Year's Eve that we would end up as such close members of the same family. My daughter has been here for half a century, and I might never have found her.'

'What would Kurt have said if he had known about this new development?' asked Agnes. 'How would he have coped with it?' I wondered what had brought about the change in Agnes's behaviour. She seemed quite affectionate again. Nonetheless, 'new development' was a curiously aseptic way to describe this volcanic emotional upheaval.

'He would have smiled his shy smile and said, I just want Agnes to be happy,' I said. 'In many ways, Agnes, he was, in the best meaning of the word, a wonderfully simple soul.'

'It seems a cruel twist of fate, Malcolm. I feel quite angry with my mother when I think of it like that. Her deceitfulness.'

'I think she wanted to protect everyone at that time. And I would have said to Kurt, Agnes was lucky to have you, and Willem for that matter, in the first five years of her life. You were a much better father to Agnes than Joe would ever have been apart from the fact that he quite simply wasn't there. Couldn't be there. She got the best of you, Kurt, and she was very, very lucky.'

'What would you have done, Agnes?' asked Joe.

And I watched as she smiled her sweetest smile at him and

said, 'That's not fair, Joe. You know I haven't got an answer to that.' And he smiled back at her and I could see a whole new world of love between them. I felt bewildered.

The reckoning came a few months later, another June and another event at Lippington House. Officially the last. The house had been sold and the family would move out in August. Josephine Sophy Stacey Snow would be christened in St Botolph's and there would be a small reception just for family at Lippington House. Sad to recount, by this time I was in a wheelchair as I could neither walk far nor stand for long. It is amazing how quickly it happens when it happens. I found it very demoralising as it made me feel even more toad-like, my legs splayed like those of the toad carcasses squashed on the road, useless dead things that they were. My fat immobilised body was more revolting than ever and I toyed with the idea of all this as a Sisyphean punishment for moral inaction. One moment you feel like an ordinary member of the human race, if a little shaky, and the next you are looking up at everybody as though you are once again a baby in a pram.

I had wondered who would collect me and imagine my pleasure when it turned out to be Elfie. She was almost nurse-like in her care for me and, after depositing me in the front seat of her new SUV, manhandled my folding wheelchair into the back of the car with impressive competence.

'Dear Uncle Malcolm, it is so good that you can join us today.'

From young woman to matronly wife in a heartbeat, I thought, as she went on, 'Theo and I are so happy together.'

I scanned her pretty little profile as she drove out of the city towards the Cotswolds.

'I have heard on the grapevine that you are moving?'

'Yes. All very exciting. We are moving with Dad and Bettina to a wonderful little village on the outskirts of Cirencester.'

'That's a very nice town,' I said automatically, although I barely knew it.

'We have a cottage with a lovely walled garden for the children to play in.'

Of course, I looked sharply at her, as she intended. 'Children, Elfie?'

'Yes, we are planning a second and in fact,' and she leant over towards me to whisper, 'I think it may be already on the way.' And she gave me a coy smile. She had no idea how this was tearing my heart to shreds, for I could see Sophy standing there on the sands, giggling and wriggling with pleasure and desire, 'You are going to be an uncle again, Mally.' And yet, and yet, I could see that possibly this was as good as life got. That baby was never born but this one might be.

'Congratulations, Elfie. I expect you are hoping for a boy this time?'

'Naturally, and we will know in advance, of course. And if it is a boy it will be Malcolm.'

'But that is a terrible name, Elfie. You can't do that to a child in these times.'

'It is a very nice name although it might be Richard Malcolm or Malcolm Richard.'

'Might it be Malcolm Richard William?'

'Yes, it might.' How very happy she is, I thought, and how powerful young mothers can be. When we got back to Lippington we met the rest of the family who were already standing at the entrance to the church. I was wheeled in and my chair placed so that I could see the newly reconstituted group, this time with their fourth member. It was the first time I had seen the baby and she certainly was a very pretty infant. I watched beautiful Theo as he cuddled the baby in his arms and thought, I could have loved you, Theo, and as if he could tell what I was thinking, he smiled back at me.

He walked over. 'Meet Josephine,' he said.

'She is a lovely baby,' I said. 'Named after her grandmother?' And I remembered what Sophy had written, '*We called her Agnes after his mother and Josephine, because I said I liked the name. Just in case, Joe.*'

'Indeed. She is truly a little miracle, is she not?'

I looked around for Agnes and saw her standing by William's

grave with Joe beside her, his arm around her shoulders. And she was gesturing around the churchyard and pointing to a flowering wild rose bush and she blew a kiss towards it. Then she turned her face up to Joe's and kissed his cheek. Something symbolic was going on, I could tell. And then she turned back towards us, looking radiantly happy.

And I allowed myself a small congratulatory thought: perhaps despite all the damage I had done I had done something good in the end.

And there she was walking over towards me, gleaming with joy. She bent down to kiss me. 'Lovely to see you here, Malcolm. Looking so well.'

So Josephine was blessed and named and we all watched with various degrees of understanding. I felt grateful to be there. After that I was pushed back to the house where I was provided with a large comfortable armchair advantageously placed on the sunny terrace.

The christening cake, saved from the wedding, was cut. I had a slice. And a cup of tea. Joe came to sit down beside me. 'Strength in numbers,' he said. 'Us elderly cousins must stick together.'

'Joe, I know it is no use but I haven't found a chance yet to say how desperately sorry I am for my silence, my unforgivable decisions about the letter. I feel mortified, as I should. I don't really expect forgiveness but thank you for sitting here with me.'

Joe looked at me, squinting a bit in the sunshine that he was facing, his handsome face tanned from a recent trip to France and for a moment my mind threw up the possibility once more that it was my sin and his virtue that preserved his physical beauty.

'Well, cousin, we could compare sins and I am not sure you would win but let's enjoy what we have. The great lesson of age. Don't look back, or not too much. You and I both feel we have messed up, but now we are family and so can I get you a drink?'

'I can't bear to think of it, Joe. I can't understand how I could not have seen what I was doing and why.'

'Why?'

'Joe, when I told Agnes of the effect she had on me as a child I think I hoped to explain something but . . . well, it did not end as I had hoped. I had thought she would view me more kindly . . . but I have since recognised in myself an unfortunate truth: that I was actually envious of my lovely kind loving sister. She left in my care the joy of her life; not just Agnes but, in Sophy's mind, her sole link with you. And I tried to keep both for myself.'

'With age comes remorse, Malcolm. There is no escaping it. However, it all depends on how you tell the story of your life. A different narrator might make you a hero.'

'Remorse for you too?'

'Of course.'

'And your sins?'

'I was extremely cruel to Clara, my first wife. I felt driven with desire by then for Molly and that felt like virtue at the time and so Clara was pushed aside. I was quite heartless. But we cannot, or should not, carry guilt around with us forever. It is not fair on anyone else. We must repent, make amends if we can, and . . . I don't know. Why are you getting me to give you a lesson in how to live, Malcolm?'

'I think I need one although I know I do not have much life left to live. Maybe that is it. Something about the end times. Do you know, Charles came to see me recently and he said he had realised that he had never been the hero of his own story and I, patronisingly, thought dear Charles, such a simple soul. But, although he has stumbled around he has been out there, doing it, living it, taking the risks, risking rejection, while I sit and smile and talk about it. The omnipotence of the disembodied story teller. This is a phrase that came to me the other night. It is the safe place in life. The raconteur, the observer. I have always claimed the role for myself. Whereas Sophy lived her life; every moment.'

'If we had met again after the war, would Sophy and I have loved each other?'

'Undoubtedly. I hope so. But then, what about Kurt? He was

such a decent guy. I want Agnes to be happy, Joe.'

'She needs uncertainty, Malcolm. She needs ambivalence and paradox to feel at ease. You must let her pursue that.'

'The post-war generation. Everything might end at the drop of a hat. They seem to feel they need to get out first. Before the world ends?'

Together we looked out over the rolling green spaces of the lawn towards the river, the current swollen with recent days of rain. From this perspective the willow cast its shadow over the water, turning brown the wavelets travelling down from the bridge with a million golden sparkling lights within them.

'Joe, do you remember Sophy? Do you remember that night? Is it fair to ask?'

'Yes, of course it is fair. I did forget her. And yet I never forgot. Ever. If you know what I mean, the memory was there, it is just that I think I tried to forget her. I did go to look for her, you know. When I got back home. Rather unsuccessfully. I went back to St Anne's Road; of course the building, hall, was gone. Probably went that night. And I remembered her name, Sophy Miller. In fact she had married by then as I now know. I remembered the Protestant father but not where his parish was. The truth is, I returned to a different country. Wars change everything. And they change the participants. There was always something hesitant, reluctant about my searches. What, after all, if we met and she had never remembered me. What a fool I would look. Or, if I found her and she remembered me but badly. Or she was just different for I knew I was different. Sophy was far braver than I was. Put her memories on the line. She believed in me. And then, if I had had the letter in 1946, it would of course have all flooded back, what then? The unlived life. The irretrievable life. I am glad she just got on with living. Married the kind and devoted Kurt: gave Agnes a good start. But, could I go back, yes, I would have returned and claimed her. A fanciful man, which I know neither of us is, might say that it was for Sophy I was looking all my life; for a repetition of that soul-searching experience when we defied death by simply . . . living, loving . . . as intensely as we could. Sophy felt to me like an other-worldly experience: a dream that gets lost in the urgency of the waking moment, the tasks, the other conversations, the million other expectations, the doctoring, the army, the bloody war, the damnable desert. And, to be truthful, the other women. But yes, I can remember this lovely young passionate girl in my arms. Of course I remember and of course it is fair to ask. Not visibly, it was dark, the blackout, and dusty, but I remember the feel of her, her warmth, her skin, her mouth, all the things that really matter.'

Then he was silent and we sat alongside each other in the small haven of privacy we had created together. After a while we returned to the mundane world of our reminiscences.

'She was a lovely girl,' I said. 'And I say that as a little brother.'

'And I remember her voice.'

'And I take it that, for the sake of my own peace of mind, you will forgive my final, shamefully late, delivery of the letter? You have missed out on what might have been years of happiness.'

'You did what you thought best, Malcolm.'

'And Agnes?'

'I am good for her. I say this with all due humility. She was showing me William's grave. She believes that I understand her feelings about that hurtful loss better than anyone else and I think that is probably true.'

'And will she be happy?'

'Well, I just think what makes her happiest is keeping her love objects at a distance. She believes they are safest there.'

'Really?'

'A bit like you, perhaps? Obviously I think this is a piece of experience she brought with her from the past.'

I could tell by his voice that he was not going to say more about it and so I simply examined the thought for myself. It seemed so obvious when he put it like this. Love objects might be kept out of harm's way at a distance. And why should we not have different styles of happiness? And, in a way, was that not all that Agnes was saying when she protested that the discovery of happiness required uncertainty? Was it? And a feeling of long-lost wellbeing filled me as I stretched out my legs in the sunshine and sipped the champagne while I tucked this question away at the back of my mind to be examined later on, when I was alone again. How good life could be. Except an uneasiness lurked in a black spot in my memory.

'Joe, she was very angry with me for keeping the letter so long.'

'Yes. She was. But you know Agnes. Always ready to fall in love, always ready to forgive. She doesn't bear grudges.'

I looked at the hill crowned with beeches, their great clouds of leaves green again. I had missed their winter grandeur.

'This will all be gone soon,' I said.

'No, it will still be here.'

'Gone for us. If a tree falls . . .'

'Someone else will be here to see this.'

'That's no good to me.'

'Nor me,' said Joe soberly.

And it was in this mood of thoughtful inebriation and gentle reminiscence that the afternoon passed most delightfully. I looked around at my family and loved them. I felt proud to be a part of them and grateful to be included.

Joe had lit me another cigarette and Richard had opened a

new bottle of champagne and was bringing it around and there was Bettina with more cake and I could see Agnes over there by the herbaceous border holding Josie up in order for her to see something. A butterfly? A flower? How pleased Sophy would have been. And I saw that Joe had walked down to say something to Agnes and then Elfie had joined them and she lifted Josie out of Agnes's arms as Theo moved towards the two of them and then Joe and Agnes turned away and walked across the lawn together down towards the sunlit river.

And as I watched her walk, her arm linked in Joe's, her face turned now to him, now towards the beech trees up on the hill, now bending to pick something from the ground before them, I realised that what I had seen in the little Agnes all those years ago that afternoon on the train was not merely some generic childish charm but something particular to Agnes: a capacity for bestowing or discovering charm, a capacity for delight that not everyone had. A preparedness to be delighted might be the best way to put it.

And I wished, how I wished, that she should be happy and yet knew alongside that how swiftly she would have mocked such a wish. 'The pursuit of happiness . . . you know I don't believe in that.' Yes, we did both know it. Apart from anything else, there was not much talk of happiness in Sophy's and my home: there was only the satisfaction of duty done. That was what counted. And then my mother and her tears, what did they mean? And there she is, fiddling with her socks and getting up from the sofa and running down the stairs towards me holding up her arms as I bend down to pick her up and as I feel my head droop forward I open my eyes to see Agnes, kneeling, crouching by my chair in front of me, looking up at me. How lovely she is, I thought, and saw as never before the clear outline of her mother's eyes and cheeks and the shape of her father's forehead.

'Malcolm. Uncle Malcolm, you were dozing off. Would you like to be more comfortable? Do you want to move inside?'

'No. No thank you my dear, I do not want to miss one moment of this afternoon.'

'We will miss this garden, won't we?'

'Does it have another worthy owner?'

'Oh, were we worthy? It was Richard's team of amazing gardeners that kept it like this.'

'But it was loved. Gardens need to be loved.'

'Yes, I have always loved it.'

'Joe thinks that is why you married Richard.'

'Well, perhaps Joe is right.'

'How is Freddie?'

'Freddie is . . . Freddie.'

'Will you see him again?'

'Of course. I love him too.'

'As I was sitting here, dreaming here, Agnes, I was imagining a conversation with you in which you were saying that we can pursue contentment but that happiness is necessarily allied to uncertainty.'

'Yes, I think I agree with that. It is when we are most alive . . .'

'May I wish you happiness, then, and all the agonies and uncertainties that come with it. And I am so, so sorry for everything. For everything, Agnes. I feel so ashamed. You do believe that, don't you?'

She leant forward and kissed my forehead and said, 'It all worked out in the end, didn't it, Uncle Mally?'

And her use of that old childish name took me, as she knew it would, back to those moments on the train when she rested her whole slight weight against my chest and I had thought it might just explode with love for her.

I found my cheeks were wet with tears I did not know I had been shedding.

'Uncle Mally, do you know why I think you were so affected by the horror you saw on my face on that dreadful morning after my mother's death? Because it was yours too. Children cannot dissimulate. You saw my unhappiness in the raw and recognised it as your own but it was the fear of it, the recognition of it, that led you to run away. To the books. To the safety. And no shame in that but, dear Malcolm, we shared our sadness then and we can share it now, can't we? For your sister, for my mother.'

She spoke with passion as she knelt next to me, as though this was a very, very important thing, and I could see she had been thinking about it and formulating the words and I accepted it as a sign of her love for me and, for the first time in my life, I began to weep uncontrollably, great sobs jerked through me and I struggled to catch my breath. I wept for Sophy, for Agnes, for my own sad life, for my terrible failures, for my feeble virtues, for my blindness, for my stupidity, for the tears of things. Something cracked, or grew, or shrank; whatever the movement was something was released, a knot was untied, a grief was named, I found that I mattered enough for my own tears to have meaning, yes, I think that sums it up. Silly but there you are, we are not complicated creatures really. Just little bundles of instincts and hopes.

'My dear Agnes,' I said as I began to recover my composure. 'You are spending too much time with a psychoanalyst.'

She mopped my cheeks with a tissue and cradled me in her arms. 'Darling Uncle Mally,' she said. And she might have been about to say something soft and gentle, but I wanted to ward that off and she could see that so she merely kissed the top of my toad-like head and walked back to the others.

And so, as though to prove that none of us knows how the story will end, it turned out that after all I did play a part in, shall we call it, my redemption? I moved for once from the edges of my life to the centre and Agnes, the beautiful, clever Agnes, with that special preparedness to grasp and to give delight, held me and comforted me and forgave me and I felt my heart move again.

Nothing has a stronger influence psychologically on their environment and especially on their children than the unlived life of the parent.

C.G. Jung

DR JOSEPH CONRAD BRADSHAW

A few weeks after Malcolm's death

MY AGNES. ALTHOUGH IT is now almost eighteen months since I have been allowed to say this with a clear conscience, I remain delighted by it. My Agnes, my beautiful daughter. Nonetheless, it is only within the privacy of this space that I would allow myself to boast like this. Hubris has always stalked me. Once Father O'Connor said very severely to me, 'Joseph, don't show off!' I had won some prize at school and felt extremely smug about it. I reported it to my kind guardian with a certain condescension and he quite rightly rebuked me so strongly that ever since I have always tried not to flaunt my good fortune. However, I can say now, quietly, my Agnes called a couple of weeks ago to tell me of Malcolm's death.

He had apparently died overnight in his sleep. Oddly enough, I had barely slept the night before for no apparent reason: it had rained throughout and I had listened to it with my usual pleasure for it always enhances my default mood of melancholia. And I had been thinking of Malcolm whom I had made a point of staying in touch with ever since our conversation at the christening. We are after all of the same tribe as well as of the same family now: old professional men with a certain accent and what was considered a good education. And we are almost neighbours, albeit on the two sides of the city, since I have now got an apartment in Grandpont, very close to where Agnes lives. Without doubt, Malcolm and I had bonded at the New Year's Eve party and then more deeply at the christening, which had represented something of a high spot for me. I had lost another wife but I had found my daughter, and, for once, I felt that my life had a semblance of respectability about it. I even had a family to belong to. I must go to see him, I had thought again last night, not knowing it was already too late, as the rain swished against the window, turning the streetlight into a kaleidoscope of shades of gold. But then rain always pushes me into a reminiscent mood and I had been looking back over the last couple of years.

I had become extraordinarily fond of my retiring, pessimistic unofficial brother-in-law and I had spent a lot of time pondering on his extraordinarily morose temperament. Early in my career I developed a theory of my own that as children we are like little bottles of varying sizes, rather like the quarter-pint milk bottles that were provided to children in post-war England (I kept this theory largely to myself, obviously), in that we each have an individual capacity to contain happiness. Sophy's capacity was large, Malcolm's was very small. There is nothing very original in this; the influence of parental and home life during the first five years is long-standing, but it was a pleasing configuration for me for it helped me understand some fundamental discontinuities between my patients at the time. A truly wonderful event would occur to them, a massive gift of fate, and yet, the capacity to absorb or experience consequent happiness would be so variable. I have concluded that it was the weight of his unrequited aspiration for joy that so held Malcolm back when it came to making decisions or indeed acting on them: I visualised him dragging a ball and chain of misery throughout his life. That weight made him unduly cautious, unnecessarily wary and, as a result, he kept Sophy's letter for half a century.

And me? My first six years blessed me with what I regard as an almost infinite capacity for happiness but I fear it has also made me greedy. And, with my sanguine temperament, I had always assumed that I would have been pleased to meet the man who was my father but now, seeing my darling Agnes dealing with the complex emotions I have evoked in her, I realise it might not have been an unmixed blessing. With everything upturned, one has to rewrite the past. What I was never able to ask my mother about, apart from his identity, was did my father know? Had he chosen to abandon me or was he an innocent, like me? But I was hardly innocent, was I? I could have searched for Sophy more diligently. I could have made her part of my story: acknowledged her as a significant part of my life. But then what? Reclaimed Agnes from her adoring father? Dear old Malcolm had treated me with astonishing respect when we met at the christening. In fact, all of my new family, courtesy once of Molly but now, significantly, Agnes, treated me as an honoured member and I had felt welcomed once again into the hallowed spaces of that opulent garden. They seemed to me to be remarkably forgiving.

It was about a week after going to Lippington for the reception and meeting Agnes that I had heard from her again. In itself that was unexpected. In the intervening days I had thought often of our conversation on the riverbank in the garden; we had, I was sure, bonded in a newly significant way. Nonetheless, despite my continuing love for her and, with hindsight, I use that word cautiously, I was entirely resolved to simply try to be a force for good in her life. The contents of her note were extraordinary. During the afternoon of the wedding reception, Malcolm had given her a letter from her mother, Sophy, written to me just after the war. She wanted to give it to me in person: could I get down to Oxford? Of course I could. By now a number of different scenarios were writing themselves in my head. I knew that Sophy must be the young girl who was nearly killed during a bombing raid in Liverpool. I had first been reminded of Sophy again by Malcolm when he talked at the wedding reception at the end of the day about his sister's life being saved by a young medic during the Blitz and I was sure I recognised the circumstances but I was puzzled by his knowledge of it. If he had had a letter detailing that encounter then it made sense. There was, I thought, only one reason why she might have written to me but why was the existence of the letter only emerging now? However, it is symptomatic of how my relationship with Molly had deteriorated, even by that point, that I did not think of rushing to her with this news but actually of making sure she did not hear of it. Benny by then was just about holding onto life in a private nursing home near Oxford and I said I was going down to visit him and then got on a train south. I chose a respectable hotel in the centre of Oxford, and gave Molly the number to defray suspicion.

It all felt curiously sleazy and brought to mind that first time that Agnes had come to my consulting room and, as I told Malcolm last year, when I said, 'The couch comes later,' despite the absolute innocence of my motives it sounded, even to my own ears, sordid, corrupt. Why had I not told Molly? And she was right. It was an old pattern. Agnes and I met in a small restaurant in the high street for lunch. She was looking, as women sometimes do when they are under stress, rather sleek and twitchy, like a beautiful greyhound. We ordered a couple of courses off the lunch menu and a pichet of red wine and began with the niceties, thank you for coming, a pleasure, how are you, etc. etc. Then she took the letter out of her handbag and placed it in front of me. 'I don't think you will recognise the handwriting,' she said. 'But this is from someone you knew once, written soon after the war.' I could hear the tension in her voice. I guessed anger and yet she was smiling at me, as though exhilarated and excited by what she was going to tell me. And at once I knew what the letter was going to say.

I opened it and read it once, then twice, and all the time I could feel her eyes on me.

Agnes leant forward. 'My mother loved you, Joe. How could you just cut yourself off?'

How could I? Indeed, how could I? I too had thought we might die that night. I had felt, as it now seemed Sophy did, that it was out of time. No consequences were possible for we were on the edge of things. There was nothing beyond. How to explain that at a different time to a different world?

But I also felt a curious sense of relief. This will seem cold-blooded but what the letter offered me was seemingly a much-postponed diagnosis. My symptoms and my associated behaviour suddenly all made sense. My obsession with Agnes, her 'terrifying familiarity'. What I called 'being in love' was then just a desperate fumbling at language to unearth the best way to describe this sense of devotion to another. How to relate to her was the question and in an attempt to define the nature of this emotion I fell back on stuff I knew all about: intimacy, fondness, neediness, hunger. I construed it sexually when all the time it was simply that all my intuitions, all my subconscious urges, were telling me this young woman was 'mine': but mine in the way a daughter is, not mine as in 'my' lover. In plebian terminology I knew she was mine but not how she was mine. I stared at her across the table, not knowing where to begin, wanting to take her hand, wanting not to alarm her by too many presumptions of intimacy, wanting to tell her I loved her, not wanting because of the absolute precariousness of the situation to say the wrong thing. What would Agnes be feeling at the moment? She appeared tense, anxious, febrile? I needed to be very careful. So while my heart thudded with a sort of glorious recognition I said, hesitantly, 'I am ashamed, Agnes, but so proud and happy to think I could be your father.'

'We need to check it out, don't we?' she said and I wondered if she was hoping that Sophy was wrong. Personally, I never doubted it. And even as we sat there, me being careful not to be too jubilant, she carefully folding the letter and replacing it in its envelope, I was reminded of my mother, who, by means of time's curious processes of prestidigitation was now also her grandmother. My memories of my mother were, as you know, tenuous in the extreme but nonetheless, now that I was permitted to make the link, she seemed to me to be re-embodied in Agnes's features and movements. And I allowed myself to recall yet again that first time that I saw Agnes when she was the age my mother was when she died and the emotions that the encounter triggered in me alongside the conviction that she was, in some sense, 'mine'.

Straight after that lunch with Agnes, I had gone back home to Molly to try, although without much hope of success, to explain at least partly the impact that Agnes had had on me which I could now understand in a different way. I confessed that I had been to have lunch with Agnes who had shown me an extraordinary letter written by her mother to me during the war. 'Sophy and I had one night together, Molly. During the Blitz. We were hiding in an empty hall together; we were both sure we would not survive the night.' I told her that as I never received the letter, I knew nothing about the birth of Agnes but that by a series of strange coincidences she ended up as my patient for a couple of years. And I emphasised Agnes's use of the word 'shining' during her therapy and how the vision of her parents wrapped in their world of joy had left her feeling.

'And I asked myself, have I ever felt that and realised I hadn't. And then somehow this changed my behaviour. Soon after that I found you or you found me?'

'And did we shine, Joe?'

'Yes we did, Molly. That night we danced and you were shining in gold, do you remember? We were shining then.'

'But it didn't last, did it Joe?'

And I had to agree. It had not lasted but, I said, 'This is the nature of things human, Molly. We can't live at that level of intensity.' Except privately I believed one could. It was just that Molly and I had failed. For some reason she even cared about my lovemaking with Sophy.

'Was she the first?'

'No, of course not. Not in those days and those times. Medical students, nurses, you know. Wars.'

'But you never forgot her?'

'Actually, I did for a while. As you know. Although I did look for her after the war, in a kind of half-hearted way. And I never talked about her.'

'Did you think about her?'

'Obviously not. But she was happy, she had a husband who loved her and she was going to have another baby.'

'And what did she think you were going to do if you turned up and found Agnes was accepted as another man's daughter?'

'I don't know.'

And this did trouble me. War is full of provisional solutions which become problems once the threats are removed. Sophy had written,

> But, Joe, I truly long for a time when we might know each other and maybe you will have a wife and I will have my Kurt but we will have shared something no-one can take from us. Is that arrogant of me?

What a fool, I thought. And yet what a sweet idealistic little fool.

And once she had extracted expressions of remorse from me, Agnes grew to be delighted. I think she had come to love the sheer drama and eccentricity of it all. 'A Victorian novel,' she said. 'Orphan finds out she is the princess of somewhere.' But after that initial attitude, which I think she partly adopted to make things easier for me, she became more withdrawn about the subject. For example, she stopped her new habit of deliberately calling me 'Dad'.

The wedding reception and its consequences had more fallout. Molly's gathering resentment finally spilled out a month or so after Agnes had shown me the letter and I had tried to explain how I felt and then one day she had asked me to leave 'the marital home' (such language a sure giveaway of a consultation with a lawyer). On what grounds? I asked. 'Oh for God's sake, Joe. How come you have to ask? Your impossible behaviour. Your totally selfish preoccupation with your own life and now your own daughter. And you even lied to me about meeting up with her, as you know. What were you thinking of? Repeating the old patterns? For Christ's sake she is your daughter not one of your bloody other women.' Or something like that. All perfectly reasonable and, what is more, true. And also, she had discovered Charles or he had discovered her, at the reception. There is nothing like a viable alternative to provoke a decision to exit a partnership. They seemed to be very well suited and I hear that she is very happy now.

And so I moved out and away from Molly and came south to my new home, Oxford. I have bought a flat in a very smart development: the rooms are small but the views are exquisite. I felt no particular distress over Molly's absence, whatever that indicates. I relished my new life and took care not to be too present to Agnes but for her to know that I would like to provide anything she needed. Malcolm had dropped a few hints as to her financial situation but she remained fiercely independent. And I made a point of visiting Malcolm as often as he seemed to want as he gradually became less and less mobile. He was clearly absolutely delighted with this new relationship between me and his niece and often said so. 'She has needed you in her life, Joe. I am just so sorry it took me so many years to see it.' And I walked for miles, the best way to explore anywhere, and befriended and was befriended and felt happy, I think, just peacefully happy for the first time in my life.

And so the days passed busily and pleasantly enough until Agnes's call a fortnight ago. Malcolm had died in his sleep, lucky bugger. A few days later I took Agnes to his funeral which was in St Ethelburga's. It was sparse enough and appropriate for a vicar's son who had long since forsworn any early faith. Agnes was welcomed by all the staff there and one or two of the other residents. At times like that she becomes weirdly regal and acts like a member of royalty. How I love her. I had been looking forward to accompanying her up to Merebridge which is where she had decided to take Malcolm's ashes; however, to my surprise and disappointment, she said no, she needed to be alone.

It is at times like this that I feel like her therapist again. I found her state of mind difficult to read and it worried me. After the funeral I drove her back home but, despite a cold wind, she just wanted to be dropped off. 'I will walk along the river a bit, Joe. Soothe my mind.'

'It was a relief to everyone,' I said. 'He was lucky to die in his sleep.'

'Yes I know. I am glad it has happened. I sometimes think I have been waiting for it.'

On my way home I thought about that statement and wondered what it meant. She did allow me to see her off yesterday and because she had some luggage and it was pouring with rain I drove her to the station to get the train north.

'Let me know if you need anything.'

'I will, Dad.' She grimaced. This was a gift. She knew it pleased me.

'Anything,' I said and she nodded. 'Anything at all,' I repeated. I waited until the train drew out and I could watch her waving through the window. She will have spent last night there and I have decided to ring her this evening. She said she might stay there for a while. She wants to visit her old haunts, Malcolm's old haunts, and go to see Sophy's grave, and Kurt's. She also wanted to walk along the sands a bit. 'Just take some time out, Joe. Revisit my past. I am sure you understand.'

'Of course I do.'

She will be back next week and she has promised to let me know which train to meet.

It is really true what philosophy tells us, that life must be understood backwards. But with this, one forgets the second proposition, that it must be lived forwards. A proposition which, the more it is subjected to careful thought, the more it ends up concluding precisely that life at any given moment cannot really ever be fully understood; exactly because there is no single moment where time stops completely in order for me to take position [to do this]: going backwards.

Journals Vol 4 l 127 1843, Søren Kierkegaard

DR AGNES JOSEPHINE STACEY

A few weeks after Malcolm's death

I AM BACK ON THE sands at Merebridge. There is a cold February wind and the savage north-easterly is driving vast black clouds overhead at speed. It is one of those days when you keep asking yourself if it is raining or not: you move through a fine mist, not quite a drizzle, but within ten yards your hair is wet and hanging damply into your eyes until the wind snatches it away again. This is the weather of my birth month and I feel at home in it. I can feel myself expand into the safety of the familiar elements, sea, wind and sky. Yesterday I caught the train from Oxford to Lime Street and then the local train to Merebridge. I had rung ahead to a small comfortable hotel near the seafront so that this morning I woke up in the unfamiliar bed to one of the familiarities of my childhood: seagulls crying and calling. It made me sad. Why am I returning to the womb, as it were, going back to a place where it is safe to feel sad? And I pause there to make a mental note: the truth is that I need a place in which it is safe enough to feel sad. I say the words out loud so that I will not forget them. But then, what is this sadness that sweeps over and under and all around me? People have said that when you look down into the grave at a burial it is your own mortality you are grieving. This is not as sophisticated as sending not to know for whom the bell tolls; this is that visceral stomach-gripping emotion one feels as death stares you in the face. It is the terror of the nightmare. But also the sympathetic response to the anguish those you loved will have felt as their end approached. My grandfather spent his life assuring people that they need not die, that they could have eternal life. This fear is not about that either: it is the process of being in transit, of everything being strange, and then I smile to myself, so that is why I have come back to Merebridge and to my known and needed elemental familiars.

Ostensibly, I have come here to mourn Malcolm. I have in the pocket of my old sheepskin jacket a small, remarkably small, cardboard box. I read once somewhere, that crematoria just burn the bodies once a day meaning that when you collect your loved one's ashes they may be mixed up with a lot of other people's. Could this be true? Did it matter?

Malcolm's funeral took place a few weeks ago just after Christmas on another suitably grey day, a damp Oxford day when the sky was overcast with unshed rain. He would have liked that weather but it was quite domestic compared with this. He loved bleak horizons although he would stretch out in the sun like a cat. As I was his next of kin, the matron in charge of his care home rang me when his heart gave out. I was at home, eating breakfast at my kitchen table. He had been found dead that morning. 'Died in his sleep, Dr Stacey. Best way to go.' I finished my coffee and toast, wondering what to do next. I hadn't even asked about the funeral. So, I rang the matron back. There would be a ceremony at St Ethelburga's as usual and then he would be cremated. They had his instructions. They asked all their residents to provide such instructions. Of course they did. After a bit more thought I telephoned Joe.

The two of us had had a difficult time since Malcolm's revelation eighteen months ago. After my initial fury with Malcolm for his unconscionable delay in delivering the letter, as I saw it, I contacted Joe and asked him to drive down to meet me in Oxford. It was a week or so after the wedding reception and one of those magical summer days when everything looks freshly painted. We met in a restaurant in the high street. It was very strange to be sitting there with my former therapist in these intimate circumstances while I handed him the letter, saying only, 'Malcolm gave me this at the wedding reception. It is from someone you once knew.' I watched his face as he read it. I saw a bit of regret, some sorrow, what I did not see was much surprise. When he looked up again he said, 'I feel ashamed, Agnes.'

'Do you remember her?'

'Yes. I do. It was wartime . . . I'm glad she had good memories. I am glad she married a good man.'

'You don't look surprised.'

'There was a group of us at the wedding reception, Agnes, sitting round the table by the footbridge, drinking whisky, talking about the war. I don't know if you remember coming to say goodbye to us; you were excited to be going home with Freddie. Malcolm had had a bit and was reminiscing about the May Blitz in Liverpool when he was only a teenager and he said that his sister Sophy nearly got killed one night. She was an ambulance driver and thus exposed to the full force of the bombs and after she was injured a young medic saved her life. I realised then it was almost certainly me and I suspected that Malcolm knew this, although I could not tell how.'

'Did you ask him about it?'

'No.'

'For God's sake, Joe. Why not? I would have done if I had been you.'

'I filed it away, Agnes. Partly, it was unbelievable and rather shocking and I needed time to think. And I did not want to ask him there, with everyone around. And I was trying to make sense of the fact that you had said nothing. By that time you had already left the reception with Freddie so I could not ask you. So maybe you didn't know either. And that was another terrible thought.' I had never seen him discomfited before.

'How could Malcolm have held onto this secret for so long?' I was feeling such a turbulent mass of feelings: still furious with Malcolm but furious too with Joe. I did not know where to find an ally. 'Why did he not say something sooner? Why didn't you say anything?'

'Fear, probably. Fear of doing the wrong thing. Paralyses all of us . . .'

And then, hesitantly, carefully, he added, 'I am so happy, Agnes, to think that you may be my daughter. I am so proud.' I looked at my old therapist who was maybe suddenly my father and both loved and hated them both. These two sides of a man who seemed to have inside knowledge of how the world worked when I had struggled so hard to be the one who knew best. Why was he not more upset over destabilising the basic assumptions of my life? Why was he not more surprised? Why was he not more apologetic?

'We need a DNA test, Joe. Obviously.' What did I hope it

would reveal? To this day, I am uncertain and in the months since then Joe and I have had many difficult conversations and my ambivalence by now is somewhat reduced. There were times when I really felt I loved Joe very much and could be grateful for his presence in my life. I had worked through the shock of first reading the letter at Lippington and my reflex fury with Malcolm and his dithering over giving me the letter. I was not surprised though; I eventually reasoned with myself that he was a daft old academic bachelor and pretty out of touch with normal human emotions. He was astonished that I was upset about it. However, Joe had made it clear that I could ask him for anything and he would do his best to provide it. And I knew Malcolm had been fond of him so, after I had spoken to the matron, I decided to call Joe. 'Malcolm has died, Joe. Suddenly, in his sleep. Do you want to come to his funeral with me?' Of course, I did not put it quite as starkly as that but I had discovered I feared being 'fathered'. It was only eighteen months since Joe had sat beside me on the riverbank at Lippington House and I had felt pleased to have a thoughtful, kind confidant who knew me very well as a new member of my extended family. I recalled the damselfly and how it had seemed to unite us in some way which neither of us bothered to spell out. And then, Malcolm's comment that he had watched us sitting side by side and seen something that made him feel we belonged to each other. But that was the problem. My life had been predicated on never belonging to anyone. Sometimes I felt as though I had to ask Joe to back off but on this occasion he accepted my invitation readily, as I had known he would, and together we decided to discourage Elfie and Theo from coming: she was very pregnant and Josie was almost unmanageable in adult settings. I had watched Elfie's child-rearing practices with a degree of alarm. Now that she was a married woman I could see increasing signs of Richard in her behaviour. She cared about the rules. She even enforced the rules. I was surprised but said little, knowing my place, as wise mothers do. It was Theo who advocated indulgence, which had always been my role when I was married. It was very curious.

'Let me collect you, Agnes. You won't want to be driving. There may be a bit of a wake.'

'If there is it will be tea and cakes,' I replied but I let him collect me in his zippy little Mercedes and so a week or so ago Joe and I found ourselves sitting there in the ancient church amongst those of the residents who had been able-bodied enough to get there. At the back were the care home staff including one sweet young girl who spoke to me afterwards. 'I am Sally, Dr Stacey. I found Professor Miller. He looked quite peaceful.' She offered me her condolences and said she would miss him. 'He was always a perfect gentleman,' she added.

I looked at her innocent face, wondering what she knew of

Malcolm, another person who had thought I might belong to him. And I felt a pang of regret that I had often been so offhand with him. On the other hand, maybe he found it easier to talk to young women. Elfie had said she had had a long talk with him at the wedding reception.

'He said he was bi, Mum. It is a striking thing when you talk to an old person and suddenly, and quite simply, the drama of their lives emerges from behind the screen of their old crumbling faces. Have you noticed that? Of course, I had worked out ages ago that he was probably gay but to hear him say this and to know that he, too, had considered the church. That was extraordinary.' I had certainly never known my uncle had considered a vocation but then I had never bothered to ask. 'And he has been so unhappy, did you know? Personally I don't think he ever got over Grandma Sophy's death but he just had no-one to talk to about it. He said that although he was grieving when she and Kurt died he was mainly just full of guilt. "Grief can feel like guilt, Elfie." That is what he said. "What did I do? What should I have done? For example, I had lent them my car. My old Morris Eight. I had checked it thoroughly but I kept going back in my mind and asking if there was more I could have done?" Clearly he kept rehearsing this and he was always a bit OCD, as you know. Well, it was obvious, wasn't it?' Was it obvious? Why then had I not noticed? Couldn't be bothered, probably.

And life had been pretty chaotic after Malcolm had dropped his bombshell: Joe's first reaction had been that we must talk about this and as I was then coming to terms with things I agreed; he had thought of moving into my spare room but that idea rapidly became intolerable since he was still my ex-therapist. After the DNA test confirmed that he was my father, I then had to go through a kind of agony as I revisited all my long-term fondness for Kurt. Joe moved back with Molly for a while (it was always her family home) but then he rented a flat in Oxford and I think really enjoyed being alone again.

I could not say Joe was not sensitive to all this: he was kindness itself knowing how confused and occasionally unhappy I was, while he was clearly just overjoyed that I had turned out to be his daughter. It was flattering of course but also (as Elfie would and did say) 'weird'. He talked a lot about the impression I made on him when he first saw me, my 'terrifying familiarity' which he put down to my resembling the mother he lost so young. The interesting issue for me is: given all the risks of unacknowledged paternity during the war, why can you not tell if someone is your father . . . or daughter . . . or mother etc. in the absence of any social confirmation? What does it say about one's sense of identity? What is the feeling of kinship once it has no social structures to rely on? Of course Joe's take was very much Oedipal and Electra complexes; he and I have acted out something. He explored all over again the complicated set of feelings he had when I was in therapy with him. 'Did I know?' he asked. 'Is that why I thought I fell in love with you? Am I sure I really did not know?' Despite my respect for him once upon a time, eventually I got very tired of these questions. From my point of view it was not a psychoanalytic issue but a sociological one. What does kinship mean? And, for us, how should our behaviour alter, if at all, now that we were father and daughter? During the funeral he kept looking at me, to see how I was. 'I'm OK, Joe,' I said. 'Malcolm and I talked about this. He knew death was close and he wanted to be alone. "No deathbed scenes," was how he put it.'

Joe had wanted to come with me to Merebridge but I forbade him. 'I need to process this alone.' His kind of language and he reluctantly agreed. So, after I had collected Malcolm's ashes from the Oxford Crematorium I brought them up north to our old home. Oddly enough the person whom I most wanted to share the news with was Freddie. Or maybe it was just that I wanted to escape from my theoretical and cerebral preoccupations and lose myself, as I always could with Freddie, in a familiar world of physical sensation. 'Just don't talk, please.'

The railings that line the promenade above the sands at Merebridge were one of the most familiar features of my childhood and I could remember climbing up their solid metal structure to stand on the lower bars when I was very small and look out at the distant coastline beyond the outline of Birsley Island. Later, but not too much later, obviously, that was where I had located my distant parents. I placed my hand on the cold solidity of its balustrade this morning and felt grateful for its continuity at a time of my own acute awareness of transience. For I have realised, belatedly, some might say, that I am mourning not just Malcolm but my mother and father, since I had been far, far too young to do so properly when they had died. This place is 'our place' and it is here I need to be to weep for them today, for as I walk along the sands the rain coats my cheeks and presses into my eyes so that I barely know what are tears and what are raindrops. It scarcely matters. I take a pinch of some sand-coloured grainy ashes, like stones rather than wispy ash, out of the cardboard box and drop them into a ridge on the sand. Almost at once they become invisible. I do it again. 'For you, Uncle Mally,' I say under my breath. 'For you dear Malcolm.' I can recall his tears at Josie's christening and my surprise at the profundity of his grief. Joe had said quite recently, 'He never got over your mother's death, you know. Never.' And I remembered how angry I had been with him because he had held onto the letter for so long. Poor Malcolm.

I had been back to visit him a couple of months ago. He had had a bit of a funny turn, as the matron put it, and he had asked for me. I drove over as soon as I could. By this time I had a full-time lecturership at Oriel where, belatedly, I had developed an interest in Leibniz and at that time was working on a monograph on his (and Locke's) first-person perspective. It was hard to put this aside since this kind of work offered many consolations, as Malcolm certainly knew; however, I am glad to say I recognised that I must make time for this. He was waiting for me when I arrived at tea-time on a beautiful November afternoon. The leaves on the beech trees in the churchyard, their solid trunks green with ivy, had fallen in coppery-coloured masses onto the grassy spaces between the old gravestones. High up in the bare branches was the bulky shape of a magpie nest. Malcolm, I knew, regarded them as his personal touchstone. He was sipping a whisky and soda which he assured me was the recommended treatment for his condition.

'What condition is that, Malcolm?'

'Age. And imminent death.'

I looked at him wondering where to go with this dramatic statement. 'Imminent?'

'Agnes, my dear, it does not matter how imminent. There is nothing else on my horizon now and I wanted to talk to you again. The last time we spoke properly was at the christening and you were quite wonderful but it was all about me and now I want to talk about you. And about final things. Would you like a whisky?'

And I surprised myself by saying I would. 'Lots of soda, Malcolm,' and he waved me towards the bottles standing on the bookcase.

'No ice, I am afraid. It is a ghastly habit anyway.'

When I had settled myself down he said, 'What do you remember of your grandfather, Agnes?'

'Plato and poached eggs, basically. He taught me about both. And he was good to me, of course, and very patient although I think I was always aware of an underlying impatience. Maybe not naturally attuned to small children? Man of his time?'

'Indeed. By then of course he had been to hell and back.'

'My mother's death?'

'Yes. Did I ever tell you that he administered the last rites to her in hospital after we had driven over to Chester?' I shook my head. 'The phone call from the hospital came as we were just starting a game of chess and he asked me to go with him. My mother stayed with you. Sophy was lying in an otherwise empty room as far as I remember. She was so pale, looked dead already, bandages around her head. But her eyes were open and she was conscious. He fell on his knees beside the bed and began to pray. I was shocked and I think she was too. He really believed, you see, he really believed everything he said when I had thought a lot of it was just his job. And then he took out of his coat pocket a small silver jar which had a consecrated wafer inside the lid and beneath that a small quantity of holy oil. He dipped his thumb into it and then stood up to lean over her and make the sign of the cross on her forehead. I saw it glistening in the light from the lamp beside her bed. I heard "Perpetual light . . . eternal rest . . . rest in peace." Sophy was looking at me. "The letter," she said.

'"I delivered it."

'"Then he'll have it." And her eyes closed. My father opened her mouth and placed the wafer in it then closed her lips again. I think she was dead by then but we stayed there, beside the bed, as my father continued to mumble his prayers. It was impressive. I saw for the first, and last, time the struggle between the man of God and the father. All this time he was weeping too and had to stop to blow his nose several times.'

'And you, Malcolm? What about you?'

'I was dry-eyed. I felt nothing except an overwhelming sense of guilt that I had lied to her. Soon after that I drove him home again but nothing, and I mean nothing in that house, was ever the same again.'

I have decided to walk the short distance along the dunes to the next town. As I walk, the damp brown sand pales and tightens with the pressure of my feet and then lapses back to its original smoothness as the signs of my footprints fade. On my left-hand side are the rust-red rocks that border the coastline.

On my right the silhouette of Birsley Island to which one can walk at low tide but not without remembering the speed with which the waves can flood the flat expanse of sand. I am walking quickly, strongly, relishing the salt smell of the air and drawing it deeply into my lungs. And as I walk, aware of the footprints I am leaving, albeit for only a moment, I remember the vision I had had at Elfie's wedding reception of my mother walking away from me on that last morning and the line of her footprints with that unmistakeably inturned left foot. She had by then been hoping that Joe had already got her letter, that they might meet soon, that she could maybe introduce me to him. I wonder who would have the temerity to judge her for that; certainly not Kurt whose nature was above all kindness itself. I wish I had known him better and longer, I wish I could have been kind to him in his old age, I wish that Joe had never turned up, that Malcolm had thrown the letter away or burned it, that they had lived to have the son they longed for. And I think, not for the first time, how surprising it was that my mother had been so accurate in her intuition that Joe is my father. How I wish I had known her. How I wish I could have loved her better and longer.

Tomorrow I will walk over to the churchyard where they are buried. I have not often seen their graves. Throughout my life, despite the eventual intellectual understanding of death, my emotional knowledge of it meant that they were not dead but merely distant, over the sea, a long way off. Such is the nature of bereavement in childhood. I have a confused memory of a pretty graveyard with in one corner a little bluebell wood which I had loved when I was taken there. And I remember creepers everywhere, although for a small person 'everywhere' does not encompass much. The grass was long but that gave the whole setting a kind of wild look that I thought I liked. However, when does wild become 'neglect'? Is it bad to neglect one's parents' graves? What happens in our nomadic worlds to graves elsewhere?

Last night in the hotel bedroom I had slept well and I had felt quickened by the salt breeze of my childhood that blew in through the open window so that I got up readily this morning and was astonished by the old face that peered back at me from the unfamiliar mirror. I am an old woman, I said to my reflection, and that is the truth. I decided not to bother with any make-up. Maybe I feel reborn. Something fundamental in me has changed. Breakfast was served in the basement and I ate the traditional eggs and bacon and toasted sliced white bread with greed and drank the sweet tea. A childhood tradition. I would find some coffee later. Then down the well-known pavements to the promenade and the sea. I am walking fast, confidently, and I open my mouth to allow the wind, laden with salt, far into my lungs. I can remember as a child walking past rows of sick old people in their bath chairs, brought here to convalesce on account of the health-giving air. This is a new start. I want a new relationship with my parents, I have decided, or with my memories of them, and with my new father, and with Elfie and her little family. I can start again, reorder my life, which has already been reordered for me by new knowledge. Pieces of seawater are lying in the ridges of sand along the long brown beach and, far out, white waves are moving slowly, imperceptibly towards the shining shallows that mark the position of the incoming tide. The gulls are becoming noisier and noisier and I can see one or two swooping down to the water's edge. I will come and live here, I say to myself. I can retire from the university and sell my little Oxford cottage and buy a small place up here with a view of the sun going down over the Irish Sea each evening. I will walk along the sands every day and I will find my parents' neglected graves and tend them and even go to the church where once my grandfather preached his interminable sermons. I can, in a very real sense, come home. And since Freddie does not belong up here I will be washed clean of him too, and I wipe the salt tears from my face as though enacting a religious ritual of my own. A new start. My shoes are squelching in the sand and I look down to see that the sea has crept up on me and I have been striding out so strongly and so swiftly that I have walked a long way. I turn around to see the distant line of the promenade and the small houses lining it and then look up to see the outline of Birsley on the right very close. In fact it looks closer than the promenade so I decide to walk as swiftly as possible towards it.

In the end, Malcolm had died alone. 'In his sleep.' But is it possible to die without knowing it? Was there not some final struggle, some final awareness? Some terrible agony when his heart could no longer find the strength to beat but simply cramped and twitched and stopped? He had said before I left on that last occasion, 'I won't send for you, Agnes. I don't want any final deathbed scenes. I want to die alone. For me it will be a solitary business; you know I have always been better alone.' And for me? What would it be like, when it came? Would it be easy? A hesitant sun is emerging through the rainclouds and far off I can see the dunes that I had been heading for. Some sense of the patterning that belongs only to me seems now to have entered my awareness; so many of the patterns that have always been mine but have been so disregarded and neglected by me are now reclaimed. Those patterns of sun on sand, sand on stone; those shadows, those movements in the spiked grasses that rattle in the wind, these interminable waves, these horizons, ineradicable memories of my childhood, they are mine. All belong to me and to me alone.

I scoop up some more of Malcolm's ashes and then decide,

since the water is now almost lapping around my ankles, to tip the whole box in. The wind catches the ashes and swirls them back across the water which now lies behind me as well. Good, I thought, I had wanted them in the sea as I thought Malcolm would have. The instructions he had left had not included what was called 'disposal of remains'. I hope he would have known I would have brought them up here. All three of them gone now: the three adults of my infancy, my grandparents long gone having moved from Merebridge when I left school, after giving me the necessary stability that far. The five adults of my childhood.

The water is freezingly cold and is beginning to fill my shoes, which are only good-quality walking shoes and not waterproof; although my grandmother would have approved of them. Does the tide really come in this fast? I have a distant memory of being told it was as fast as a horse could gallop. I am much closer to Birsley now and as long as the sand between me and the island is flat I am confident I can reach it in time. I feel happier and stronger than I have for a long time. I know I can do it. Feeling joyously unkempt, unwashed, I splash towards the island, battered by the wind that rushes in off the wave-driven sea. I feel indomitable. I smile as the wind tugs at my clothes and blows my hair across my face. It strips me of my identity, my name, my past, and I know that something I cannot define has been regained by this visit to my old home. Because I cannot define it I cannot share it and therefore I can, perhaps, not lose it either; it is a part now of that incommunicable sense of myself which is so vivid a constituent of this day. The island is now really quite close and there are the rocks not far ahead of me. Once I get there I will surely be safe and all I will have to do is to wait for the tide to go out again. I am moving forward as fast as I can with the water almost up to my knees. I can do it. I know I can. But I mustn't fall over for then I will struggle to stand again in the swift currents that now flow all around me. So close. Nearly there. I reach my hand out towards the rocks. My feet are numb now and moving them has become increasingly difficult. I am shivering violently in the extreme cold and my hair is blowing all over my face so that I can barely see where I am going. But never mind. I am nearly there. Very nearly there. So very nearly there.

ACKNOWLEDGEMENTS

I was born in the same year as Agnes and, like her, spent my early years on the west coast of England beside the Irish Sea and, like her, as an adult I have been entertained in the beautiful garden in Gloucestershire. There all resemblance ends, since I grew up in Central Africa and my own mother died in her late eighties and my father soon after and so, for the avoidance of all doubt, I need to acknowledge that the characters in this book are entirely fictional. Nonetheless, like many born at that time, I have been nurturing this post-war novel ever since.

I owe the fact that I have a two-book contract to my remarkable agent, Eleanor Birne at PEW Literary and thus an obligation to write a novel once *Cat Brushing* had been published and I seized the chance. If it had not, however, been for the timely inspirations of Jon Riley and the firm hand of Jasmine Palmer in London and the constant encouragement of Elisabeth Schmitz in New York this novel would have remained a sad stillborn thing.

As a non-academic I have also relied heavily on Dr Severin Schroeder for his generous advice regarding the fictional Oxford academic careers of both Agnes and Malcolm.

Finally, I have relied on the steady support and interest of my four children and their partners in Bermuda who have, I am sure, been discussing this new book and wondering what on earth I am going to come up with this time.

Oxford 2023